Midnight Sun

MJ Fredrick

Copyright © 2012 MJ Fredrick
All rights reserved.
ISBN: 1463631928
ISBN-13: 978-1463631925

DEDICATION

To the Wet Noodle Posse, who helped me believe

CHAPTER ONE

Brylie Winston gathered her clothes as quietly as possible in the darkened hotel room in Hobart, Australia, one eye on the man sprawled on his stomach in the center of the king-sized bed. Light from a part in the curtains fell over the bed, illuminating his muscled shoulders and back, jaw shaded with stubble around a sensuous mouth, and those long eyelashes that were always her downfall. Her stomach churned with regret even as her skin tingled with memories of his touch.

What had she done? She never let herself get carried away by a sexy man with a charming accent who clearly just wanted to get laid. She'd learned her lesson about that the hard way. But her gaze riveted to Marcus the moment he sauntered into the bar and when he'd approached, well, she'd been helpless. She hadn't had sex in so long—hadn't felt sexy in so long, she'd bought into his flirtation, his casual touches, his proximity as the bar got more crowded. She let herself be seduced, escorted here, and very, very thoroughly made love to.

Her body heated as she recalled his expert kiss, his callused hands that melted her clothes away.

And then it got good. Her body hummed with the desire for a repeat, but waking him up opened up way too many dangerous possibilities, the worst of which—more rejection. Yeah, she didn't need that, not after New York.

Which was why she was now on the other side of the planet.

Snatching her jeans against her chest, she tried to shake some sense back into herself. She slipped into the bathroom and dressed quickly in the dark, pausing only at the odd fit of the jeans. Hoping she wouldn't wake him, she flipped on the light to see the Levi's tag on the back pocket. She'd grabbed his instead.

She caught sight of herself in the mirror, and her fingers went to the beard-burn at her throat before she finger-combed her rat's nest hair. God, was that a—no, not a hickey, just a shadow. Thank God. That would hardly look professional above her chef uniform.

She turned off the light and crept back into the bedroom. He grunted and shifted in the bed, and she froze. She didn't want conversation—she wanted last night to be a memory.

A bone-melting, no-other-man-could-live-up-to memory.

Time to go. She yanked on her own jeans, crammed her feet in her boots, felt her way across the dresser until she found her purse, and beat it out of the room.

Marcus Devlin arrived at the Hobart dock and tightened his grip on the strap of his duffel as he looked up at the Ice Queen. The Russian icebreaker had been converted to a cruise ship for people who would pay a pretty penny to see Antarctica up close. His family's travel company had made a fortune from the greenies who wanted to see the unspoiled land, but Marcus never had the desire.

Still didn't. But after his latest scandal, his family insisted he occupy his time in a more productive way and learn how the family business was run. Plus, sending him to the end of the earth had been an idea they'd threatened for years now, although with less specificity than this.

How was he supposed to know the asshole whose nose he broke in the bar fight was a senator's son? Though now that he looked back on it, it explained a lot. The prick.

So, yeah, he wasn't in jail, but Christ. He shuddered. That might almost be preferable.

He straightened his shoulders and headed up the ramp, grateful at least that this cruise ship didn't have fancy dress dinners or balls like the other cruises his family owned. There wouldn't be any expectation he act as someone he wasn't.

He glimpsed a flutter of red hair below him and whipped around, wondering if it was the girl who'd slipped out of his bed this morning. The twist amused him—he was usually the one doing the sneaking. That the girl had beaten him to the punch threw him off balance.

But no, he couldn't be that lucky. Despite her initial shyness, she'd been amazing once he got her to his hotel room, so open, and the combination had been freaking sexy. He planned to look her up when he got back into port. Of course, he hadn't gotten her number, so it might not be easy.

He crossed the deck, wondering where the hell the pilothouse would be, if the captain was there or somewhere else. From what he'd been told, they wouldn't be taking on passengers for a couple of hours, plenty of time for him to introduce himself to the captain, find his berth and hide for the next two weeks. He had to be on this boat. He didn't have to like it.

That flash of red again, this time closer. He turned to follow, and damned if it wasn't her, right here on this ship. Gorgeous titian hair pulled back in a thick, soft-looking ponytail—last night at the bar it'd been down around her shoulders, and when he'd gotten her in bed, well, it'd been—yeah, best not to pursue that. Soft white skin, full pink lips—best not to think of those, either—lush body hidden beneath layers of clothing, the sweatshirt she wore now proclaiming her "Ice Queen" when he knew she was anything but.

Right. The name of the ship. She worked here? Christ, was he her boss? A chuckle escaped, drawing her attention in his direction. She went absolutely still, then absolutely red. Desire zinged through him at that innocent blush, especially when he had intimate knowledge that she wasn't all that innocent.

"Morning," he said, approaching. She cast a glance over her shoulder at the rail and for a moment he thought she considered jumping overboard to get away.

"Morning," she replied instead, backing up.

Oh, yeah, he liked this game. Big Bad Wolf and Little Red Riding Hood. "I didn't think you'd be gone when I got up."

"Thought you'd beat me to the punch?" she retorted with a swish of her ponytail.

Little Red had teeth. Well, he knew that, sort of, but appreciated the bite of her observation nearly as much as the scrape of her teeth on his skin. "You got me." His gaze flicked to her breasts and the words printed across them. "I beg to differ."

Her shoulders stiffened. "The ship."

"You work here?"

"I do. You're a passenger?"

For a moment he considered saying yes, hiding who he was, but he was never very good at pretending. "I'm the youngest Devlin."

She drew in a sharp breath, clearly recognizing the name. "You own the ship."

"Yeah. Well. Not me." He didn't own much of anything, to be honest. Too much responsibility went along with that.

"We've never had an owner on a cruise."

That statement, almost an accusation, intrigued him. He resisted the urge to lift his fingers to her soft cheek as he asked, "You've been on a lot of these?" He expected the crew to be more rugged and outdoorsy, not with a peaches and cream complexion.

"I've worked for you for two years."

He grinned and rocked back on his heels, needing to get some distance from her before he did something stupid, like touch her. "The I suppose you know where I can find the captain."

She nodded and pointed down the deck. "He should be there in the pilothouse, the last doorway as you approach the bow."

He stared at her. Crap. His brother Harris had told him he needed to learn the lingo, but as usual, he'd blown it off. So he did what he always did when he didn't understand. He gave her his most charming grin. "Show me?"

She opened her mouth to protest, then apparently recalled that he was her boss. She squared her shoulders and led the way across the deck.

"So what is it you do here?" His hand tightened on his duffel as he watched the sway of her ass in those snug blue jeans. "I thought you said you were a student."

She frowned over her shoulder. "I didn't say that. Must have been one of your other conquests."

Hey, that was uncalled for. He trotted up to walk alongside her. "No, you said you were a student. The name of the school sounded swank." He sought his memory, which had admittedly been impaired last night as he drank to forget he was heading out to sea today. And to forget the pain he was leaving behind. "Culinary school. That's it. You go to a culinary school in New York."

"I did go. Past tense." Her cheeks pinkened, then she slowed and turned toward an open door. "The captain is right through there."

Marcus wasn't ready to let her walk off yet. "Won't you introduce me?"

She huffed an exasperated breath. "Are you going to be this difficult the entire trip?"

"Depends."

"On what?"

"On you."

She folded her arms and faced him. "So if I'm nice to you, you'll go easy on us?"

"If you're nice to me, I'll go easy on you," he corrected.

She waved an exasperated hand and pivoted to walk into the pilothouse.

The place was all polished cherry and chrome, with huge windows on all sides, and more gizmos tucked into the paneling than Marcus could name. Harris probably had fun with all this—he was a long-time geek, especially when it came to technology. A big man—and he did mean big, six-six if he was an inch, and built like Hagrid from the Harry Potter movies—turned from the controls when he heard them come in.

"Brylie!" He enfolded her in a bear hug that had her shoulders go stiff, and Marcus took a step forward to intervene, since the embrace obviously made her uncomfortable.

"Dad," she said, breaking free.

Marcus stared. No, he couldn't have heard that right. Not only had he slept with the chef on the cruise ship his family owned, she was also the captain's daughter? And this guy looked like he'd throw Marcus overboard at the slightest provocation.

"Dad?" he repeated, but she didn't meet his gaze.

So Marcus turned to the big man, whose face was hidden by hair a shade darker than Brylie's, who had the same blue eyes. Oh, hell.

"Dad, this is Marcus Devlin. Did you know he was joining us on this cruise?"

She spoke like butter wouldn't melt in her mouth, and Marcus began to rethink the appropriateness of her sweatshirt.

"I had heard," her father, the captain, said. Captain what? Marcus didn't remember getting her last name. Hell, for half the night, he'd called her Riley. The captain thrust a hand out at Marcus. "Captain Winston. And you've already met my girl Brylie. Best chef you have in your fleet. Trained in New York at some of the best restaurants."

Instead of looking proud of this accomplishment, she kept her gaze averted. She didn't want to be here, Marcus realized. She wanted to be at one of those restaurants. So why wasn't she?

He was a sucker for mysterious women.

"Speaking of," she said, her voice brisk. "I need to get to the kitchen to get tonight's dinner started. The passengers won't like to be kept waiting."

"Mr. Devlin's cabin is on the way to the galley." Her father's voice boomed off the windows. "Why don't you show him to the VIP Suite? I'm sure he'd like to get settled before he tours the ship."

Her cheeks grew pink again, and she didn't look at him, but nodded. "Of course. I'll see you after dinner." She stretched up to kiss the big man's cheek, then motioned for Marcus to follow her.

"He's going to break me into pieces, isn't he?" Marcus asked when, instead of leading him back onto the deck, she led him through a door to an interior hallway.

"There's no reason for him to know what went on last night." She glanced over and he saw just the hint of a humor in those gorgeous blue eyes. "Besides, you have your name to protect you."

Of all the beauties in Hobart, he had to seduce this one. Too soon to tell if she was going to make his trip exciting or miserable.

"Here's your cabin." She motioned to a door on her left. "Do you have your key card?"

He did, and fumbled for it before sliding it in the lock and swinging the door open.

"Suite," the captain had said, but the room was half the size of the hotel room from last night. The room he stood in contained a sofa and a desk in the corner. The windows were shuttered along one wall.

"Bed and bath through there." Brylie pointed to a door in the paneling. "Enjoy."

"Wait." He grasped her arm and pulled her into the room with him, then opened the door she indicated. A queen-sized bed took up most of the area, barely giving him room to walk around it. He popped open another door leading to the tiniest bathroom he'd ever seen. So much for his plan to hide out in here for the duration. He'd lose his mind. "This is the VIP suite?"

"You have complete privacy," she said. "Most of the other passengers pay a pretty penny and still have to share a bathroom with strangers."

"Cozy," he murmured.

"Well, these ships are converted icebreakers, not designed like your other ships. Besides, most people don't stay in their rooms very much. There's a beautiful lounge up on Deck Five, where they can watch the ocean and see the icebergs and occasional wildlife. Most people come on these trips to be social."

She was watching him with an unnerving accuracy. Did she read his mind? OR was she wondering at his real reason for being here?

"Will you take me on a tour later? After dinner, maybe?"

"I'm very busy, Marcus. We have two hundred passengers and crew, and my responsibilities lie elsewhere."

"You don't work in the kitchen alone, surely."

"I have a crew," she admitted. "But my name is at stake."

Right. She'd play hard to get, now. So he'd play the boss card. "And I'm your employer."

This time she went beyond pink to red. Fury sparked in her eyes. "You have plenty of other minions to wait on you. Sir."

"I don't want anyone else. I want you." He was being stubborn and unreasonable. But he wasn't accustomed to settling.

"There won't be a repeat of last night," she said, her voice prim. Ice Queen, indeed.

"Why not? You had fun."

She didn't rise to the bait, and he hid his disappointment when she capitulated.

"Fine. At nine, after dinner, I'll show you the ship. I won't be free before then, so don't ask."

He nodded, already missing the battle. "Right. Nine o'clock, then."

When she turned to stalk off, he determined she'd definitely be making his trip more exciting.

***

Brylie smacked the ladle against the side of the pot with more force than necessary, drawing the attention of her crew, and waving it off with an impatient hand.

This. This was why she didn't make rash decisions. This was why she made plans and followed them to the letter.

This was why she hadn't had sex in a year and a half.

How had she let herself be seduced by a handsome Aussie with stories of a carefree life, of his travels, a man living his dreams? She should have known better. But he'd made her feel desirable as a man hadn't in years, and while part of her brain told her he probably did the same to all the girls, her neglected side bought his seduction hook, line and sinker.

Now they were stuck together on this suddenly-too-small ship for the next twenty days, and he wasn't above using his clout—she'd slept with the owner, good Lord—to get his way.

Worse, her body remembered him all too well and wanted a replay of last night. He'd been very, very attentive. And he'd made her laugh and feel good about herself, and—feel good. Something that hadn't happened in a long time.

Then he'd fallen asleep and she'd been alone with her thoughts and fears and she'd beat it out of there, thinking she could put it behind her.

The only thing to do was keep him at arms' length, do what he asked for the sake of her father and her own job, but make sure he understood this was only professional.

***

Marcus sat at the captain's table, not nearly as grand as the ones on the other ships in the fleet, but that suited

Marcus fine. He wasn't much for tuxedos and champagne, for ballroom dancing and diamond cufflinks, much to the dismay of his family, who considered him a changeling.

More passengers were on board than he expected. Sixteen tables with a dozen at each table, not including the crew. He observed the differences in the people at his own table: four young men who had come for the adventure, wanting to say they'd ridden a kayak on the Southern Ocean, an older Hispanic couple who were both teachers and had been saving for this trip for a long time, a big man traveling alone, which Marcus thought odd, and a family of three—mother, father and sullen preteen boy. Marcus probably had most in common with the boy, who didn't seem to want to be here anymore than Marcus did.

He listened to the conversation flowing around him, sipping the Antarctica beer served with the delicious lobster risotto and flaky bread. Brylie was excellent at her job. He couldn't help picturing her in one of those puffy hats and nothing else—well, maybe an apron. Definitely an apron.

"—seen any pirates in these parts?"

Marcus snapped his head up and looked at the big fellow down the table who asked the question, eyes bright with anticipation. "Pirates?" he scoffed.

"Yeah, sure, like off Somalia. You heard about that, surely?" the dark haired man countered.

"That was a merchant ship," Marcus pointed out, sitting forward to set his empty glass on the table. "Supplies that could be sold."

"Right," Captain Winston jumped in. "Nothing to worry about here. Too cold for pirates down here, anyway."

"That's not what I heard," the other man said, shoulders set stubbornly. "I heard these waters aren't patrolled well, especially as winter approaches. I'm just wondering at the danger."

The comment set off ripples of alarm around the table. Marcus took in the upset expressions on the faces of the women in particular and turned back to the antagonist, tension tightening his muscles as he fought the urge to pound the man into the carpet.

"So what's your point, mate? You want to see pirates, is that it? Or do you want to upset all the good folk here who just want to see a few penguins?"

The other man scowled. "I just want to know how safe I am."

"Likely you should have looked into that before we set sail, then, eh?" He didn't wait for a response, but leaned back and signaled to the waiter for another beer. "Oh, and hey, tell Miss Winston I want to see her."

The waiter nodded briskly and hurried back to the kitchen.

Sure, if he was going to antagonize one, may as well antagonize another.

***

Brylie's stomach tightened when her head waiter, Damian, poked his head in the kitchen.

"One of your passengers wants to speak to you."

She reached behind her for the ties of her apron. "Is something wrong?"

Damian shrugged. "Not as far as I can tell. Some tension in there, though."

She set the apron aside and pushed through the swinging door into the full dining area. Without thinking, she scanned the room for Marcus and saw him immediately, looking straight at her.

"That one," Damian said, gesturing to Marcus, confirming her suspicion.

She huffed out a breath, put on her professional face, and strode to his table. He was sitting with her father, damn him, so she had to be on her guard. She stopped a few feet away and folded her hands in front of her.

"Is everything satisfactory?" she asked.

"Everything is amazing," he replied. "Where did you get this Antarctica beer?"

Her shoulders tightened. He was playing with her, of course. She could see the glint in his eyes. "It's actually made in Brazil."

"Clever." He kept his gaze—had she noticed his eyes were blue?—steady on hers. "You didn't attend the mandatory lifeboat drill this afternoon."

He'd been looking for her? That shouldn't send any kind of thrill through her. She'd already shown she didn't have good judgment where he was concerned. "I know the drill."

"You never know if there's something you might have missed in the past. This does seem to be a bit riskier than, say, a cruise in the Caribbean."

She lifted her eyebrows. "I'm aware."

He folded his arms on the table and gave her the grin that had charmed her right out of her panties. "I probably could use some tutoring. Perhaps some practice getting in and out of the boat."

Her face heated. Her father was watching and had to understand what was going on, at least on one level. She had to deflect Marcus's interest. "The captain can probably arrange for Josh to help you."

He sat back, the teasing light fading from his eyes. "Josh. Big guy? Missing teeth?"

She nodded. "Former hockey player. You met?"

A frown creased his brow, making her wonder about that encounter. "We've met."

She rocked back on her heels, wanting to retreat into her kitchen. "Is there anything else?"

He leaned forward. "What's for dessert?"

She pretended not to pick up on his meaning. How was she going to extricate herself from this without losing her temper? She'd worked hard to keep a stranglehold on it, but now it was slipping its leash. "The chocolate torte is the best tonight."

"That you made yourself?"

"My baker, actually. Would you like some?"

"Which is your favorite?"

She was aware of her father watching Marcus with thunder in his expression. She kept her expression implacable, her hands folded in front of her. "The crème brulee is my favorite."

"Not the chocolate. I pegged you for a chocolate girl."

She would not react to his reference to the chocolate martinis from last night. "Crème brulee is my choice. Is there anything else I can do for you?"

He sat back in his chair. "Just don't forget your promise to give me a tour when you're done."

She nodded and turned away, aware of his attention on her as she spoke to the other guests, collecting compliments and promising recipes. She heard her father draw Marcus's attention with a question about Devlin's Alaskan cruises, and she made her escape, back into the safety of her kitchen.

He was going to make her life miserable. Maybe she should just tell her father what had happened last night, but Marcus was right. Her father would break him in half and feed him to the whales. He might be irritating, but he didn't deserve that. He didn't seem to have the self-preservation gene, though. What was he thinking, flirting with her like that?

"He likes you," Monica, her assistant chef, observed when Brylie ducked back into the kitchen.

Brylie determined not to linger on how high school that sounded. "You were watching?"

Monica rolled her big brown eyes. "Honey, he's hot. I've been watching him since he boarded."

"He's our boss."

Monica stretched to look past her. "He doesn't seem very boss-like."

Brylie made a noncommittal noise and returned to the plating area. She hoped Monica didn't figure out that the two of them had been intimate. The woman couldn't keep a secret for love or money. And she was way too observant for Brylie's comfort. She'd definitely notice that Marcus chose her to show him around the ship. She had to downplay that for her own peace of mind.

***

Marcus waited on the deck, leaning against the rail, when Brylie found him, ten minutes after their agreed meeting time. He turned with a scowl.

"Bloody cold out here." He slapped his hands on his chest. "Where've you been?"

"Working. And if you'd met me in the lounge like I suggested—"

"You wanted to meet me outside the lounge. I got the feeling you didn't want to be seen with me. Hiding from your daddy, or maybe Big Josh?"

Her nostrils flared, which she immediately regretted. It *was* damned cold out here. "Not wanting anyone to think there's something here that there isn't."

He stroked a gloved finger down her cheek. She stepped out of his reach, though every nerve in her body wanted to lean in and rediscover last night's pleasure, her skin tingling with the memory.

"I thought I made it clear," she said instead.

He eased away and grinned. "I like to watch you blush. It reminds me of—"

"Stop that. I mean it, Marcus." She set her mouth in a frown. "That wasn't something I ordinarily do, and I don't want it affecting my job."

"Why did you do it, then?" Despite his claim of being cold, he made no move away from the rail.

"You were just that charming," she said to end the line of questioning, drawing a scoffing laugh from him. "Would you like to see the ship, or not?"

He stretched his hand in front of him, palm up. "Lead the way."

She led him up a level to the social deck, where the lounge contained dozens of low-backed chairs, some angled together, some toward the windows that lined the walls, floor to ceiling.

"If you're cold, this might be the best place for you to watch the whales and icebergs," she said. "The glass is well-insulated, so the room stays comfortable, as long as you're wearing warm clothing."

"I don't mind being cold when I'm not waiting for someone. I am a snowboarder, after all."

She slanted him a glance. "I thought that was just something you said to get laid."

Amusement quirked his lips. "Well, yeah. But it also happens to be true."

She would not let him amuse her. Hadn't that—and the chocolate martinis—brought down her resistance last night? "Down here, we have a theater and lecture hall. We have two biologists, an ornithologist and a climatologist on board who do scheduled lectures, in exchange for the opportunity to travel to Antarctica three or four times a year. The schedule is in your room if you're interested."

"Yeah, I'm not much on lectures." He gave the well appointed, theater-seating room a cursory glance.

"You should never stop learning," she chided in her best schoolteacher voice. If only he wasn't so much fun to tease.

"Yes, Mother." He followed her past the library, which she assumed he'd have less interest in. "Who's the bloke who was getting everyone worked up about pirates at dinner?"

"I heard about that. I don't know."

"I told him to bugger off but I've been thinking about it. He's not right, is he?"

"We get warnings, just the same way we get warnings about sea ice and the like. It's very rare to see another ship out here. Don't worry your pretty head. Now, would you like to see the waste management system?"

His grin flashed, white teeth and gleaming eyes. "Pretty sure the answer is no there. What about the kitchen?"

She stiffened. Her sanctuary. "That's off-limits to passengers."

"But I'm the owner," he reminded her unnecessarily. "I want to see your set-up, see if there's anything I can do to make your job easier."

"You might consider jumping overboard," she said sweetly, and led the way to the kitchen.

***

One might have thought she was leading him into her bedroom, the way she tensed when they walked into the kitchen. What exactly did she think he was going to do? No, she wasn't scared of him. Scared of herself, maybe.

The kitchen was spotless, lots of stainless steel, a place for everything and everything in its place. He expected no less, from what he knew of Brylie. She showed him her side-by-side ovens and giant dishwasher and a stove big enough to cook an entire whale on. She showed him the walk-in freezer—a bit redundant considering where they were. The arrangement seemed pretty chaotic to his untrained eye, but she explained the process and he had a sudden longing to see her in action.

"Are you responsible for every meal? I mean, do you get down here at the crack of dawn to get breakfast going, or does someone else do that?"

"Someone else, but for the first few days of the cruise I like to pop in and make sure everything's running just so."

"It's the librarian thing."

She looked at him sharply. "I'm not a librarian."

"Right, I know, but it's the need for order, right? I mean, everything in here's perfect. Of course you'd want your people to be as close to that as possible. I get it." Boy, was he off if he thought she'd go for him again. He was about as far from perfect as one could get. And he certainly wasn't one she could order around.

Which only made this more of a challenge. He did like challenges.

"So you trained in New York. Didn't you like it?"

Something shifted in her eyes, darkened. "I loved it."

"Yet you're here on the open sea. Do you love that, too?"

She fiddled with a towel folded neatly on the counter. "It's an adventure, always meeting new people, seeing a part of the world so few people see."

"You didn't answer my question."

She leveled a look at him. "I miss New York."

"And you're not there because?" The tension in her body made him believe she wouldn't tell him.

She shook her head. "Too many mistakes."

He tried again. "Not your cooking, surely?"

"Personal," she said shortly, and snapped her spine, preparing to dismiss him, no doubt.

"Where's your cabin? Or do you share with your daddy?"

She narrowed her eyes and her full lips thinned. "I have my own cabin, but I'm not telling you where."

He angled his head. "Ah, I don't go anywhere unless invited. You know that."

"But you do have a broad definition of invitation," she said.

"Sweetheart." He took a step closer, essentially trapping her between the dishwasher and another counter. "You invited me."

Her gaze riveted on his mouth and he saw the desire there, recognized it from last night. "I'm not inviting you now."

"Oh, yes. You are." He dipped his head close enough to taste her breath on his lips when she pushed his chest, sending him back a step.

"No. I'm not." Her voice was a little breathy, and that should have gratified him, except she slipped past him and headed for the door. "Lock up when you're done here."

Well, hell. He hadn't read those signals right at all.

***

Marcus spent most of the next day keeping an eye out for the sly redhead and avoiding conversation with her father. He didn't trust himself to keep off the topic of

Brylie and what she'd run away from in New York. Instead, he hung about with the passengers in the lounge, where the topic of excitement was the possibility of seeing whales migrating. Marcus was no great animal lover, but he did love creatures of power, and hell, whales were the biggest animals in the world. The binoculars kept him occupied for about, oh, a half hour, then he had to move. He wanted to venture into the kitchen, but he'd seen the sharp knives Brylie kept in there. Probably not the best choice. So he bundled up to stroll the deck.

"Hey, aren't you Marcus Devlin?" A young blonde woman he'd noticed at dinner last night—he was a man, and a dog, to boot—approached him, shivering a bit in her brand new parka. "The snowboarder?"

"Yeah, I am." Even three years after he'd won the Olympic bronze, he felt pride in his accomplishment. And at least it wasn't another question about pounding that guy in the face back home.

"I'm Trinity. You were awesome. You totally should have gotten the gold."

He grinned. "I can't argue with you there."

"Do you still snowboard?"

"Not the half-pipe anymore. Just the downhill."

"Are you trying out for next year?"

"Nah. I did what I wanted to do."

"So what are you doing now?"

That was the question, wasn't it? He needed to find an answer to it, or end up like poor Jordie. "Learning the family business, it seems."

She took his meaning immediately. "This is your family business? I didn't know you were rich."

Aha. His guard came up, then. "Not me. My family. And I'm the youngest, so the farthest out of the loop."

She waved a dismissive hand. "Right. I get that. My father already told me my older brother's going to inherit so not to expect anything more from him than a college education."

Whoops. Alarm bells went off at that, and he looked closer. Was she a—?

"Are you in college now?" he asked, in what he hoped was a casual tone.

"Wilmington Prep," she replied promptly.

Christ. High school. Time to get back into the lounge, to the safety of numbers. "The cold down here is nothing like the cold in the mountains," he said, walking back to the door. "Let's go back in, shall we?"

Relief started to relax his muscles as he opened the door into the lounge, but Trinity leaned her shoulder into his chest playfully. He looked up then, straight into Brylie's blue eyes.

CHAPTER TWO

Brylie met Marcus's eyes over the head of the little blonde, and he jerked his hands up as if to signal he'd done nothing wrong. She shook her head and turned back toward the kitchen.

Rapid footsteps approached.

"Nothing happened."

She turned to give him a quizzical glance. "What?"

"I didn't know she was a teenager. I didn't even know she was out there—she came out after I did."

She stopped just outside the kitchen and turned to face him, folding her arms in front of her. "Why do you care what I think?"

"I—care." He furrowed his brow as if the question puzzled him as well.

"Because you think I believe what happened between us was special? Out of the ordinary? Believe me, Marcus, I have no illusions."

He opened his mouth to say something, but she held up a hand.

"Don't lie to me, Marcus. At least have that much respect."

She walked into the kitchen, hoping he wouldn't follow. She didn't understand why he was still pursuing her. She understood it was a one-night stand and didn't want anything more, especially here. She knew he was no stranger to one-night stands, so was it just convenience that had him after her? He thought since she'd given in once, she would again?

She didn't have time to deal with it. Time to get back to work.

***

Brylie woke up when her room phone rang. She rolled over, rubbing her eyes, and answered.

"I need you in the dining room," her father said over the line, his tone brisk.

Brylie sat up, instantly awake. "Why? What's going on?"

"We were issued an alert."

"Weather?" Mentally, she started battening down her kitchen, though for the most part it was designed for such an event.

"Pirates."

Her heart kicked an extra beat and she swung her legs over the edge of the bunk. "I'll be right there."

She hung up and reached for her jeans. An alert. That meant next to nothing, usually, but they'd never had a pirate alert before. Her father no doubt wanted to go over procedure. At least she hoped that was why he was calling them in at—she glanced at the clock—four in the morning. She tugged on socks and shoved her feet in her sneakers. She snatched up her Ice Queen sweatshirt and headed out the door.

The majority of the crew had gathered in her dining room, at the table close to the windows. Her father paced in front of them, and Monica gestured for Brylie to join her at the seat next to her. Brylie started forward, but a noise behind her drew her attention.

Marcus padded down the hall behind her, barefoot, scrubbing his hands over his face. She stopped herself from reacting just in time. Of course her father would want him here. He was an owner. Before he met her gaze, she scurried over to the seat by Monica.

That didn't deter him. Oh, no. The arrogant bastard grabbed a chair and dragged it through the others who were already seated, bumping feet and legs out of the way, and sat beside her. He flashed a quick grin, stretched his legs in front of him, folded his hands over his stomach, and turned his attention to her father. On her other side, Monica nudged her, but Brylie ignored her, knowing she would just get those raised eyebrows—or worse, a waggle. If Monica figured out her secret, it would be all over the ship.

Her father stopped, scanned the crowd and cleared his throat. The room instantly silenced.

"We received an alert from Southern Ocean Patrol that there is a suspicious vessel in the vicinity, last seen off the southeast coast of New Zealand. We don't know what their destination is but they refused to answer a hail."

"That doesn't necessarily mean anything, does it?" Joan Seward, the ship doctor, asked, shifting in the wooden chair, drawing her legs tight against the seat.

The captain lifted a shoulder, trying to be nonchalant, but Brylie knew him too well. He was concerned, or he wouldn't have called them in this early.

"They're heading due east, which is why it's an alert only. I just thought it would be best to go over our procedures, since this is new for us."

"You have pirate procedures?" Marcus straightened beside her. "Have you ever encountered pirates?"

"We've never even had an alert as long as I've worked on the Ice Queen," her father replied. "I don't want anyone to be alarmed, but I do think it's time to refresh. The first thing in event of a suspicious vessel is to get the passengers to the interior of the ship. Our ship is somewhat easier to board than a normal cruise ship because we don't have the high firewall, and we don't have as many resources as the bigger ships do, which makes us a better target. We don't have as many people, either. We do have high-pressure hoses in event of a boarding, and our security force is armed."

"How big is your security force?" Marcus leaned forward now, alert.

"We have six men who work in shifts, four automatic weapons and half a dozen handguns."

"Against pirates."

"Which we've never had to deal with and don't expect to deal with now," her father reminded them all in a chiding tone. "I'm only going over procedures. We take evasive maneuvers if we can. The Queen isn't particularly nimble, and the seas here can be rough, but she's steadier than a smaller ship in these waters. Also, she's an icebreaker and can go places a smaller ship can't. So our first step is of course to avoid them. Secondly, if they manage to disable us somehow, we turn the high-pressure hoses on them. One thing no one wants is to have the icy water of the Southern Ocean blasted at him. Should that fail, we have the weapons."

"And if that fails?" Marcus asked.

"Then we pray the Southern Ocean Patrol received our distress call and can get to us. It's a lot of defense, Mr. Devlin."

"But you still felt the need to call this meeting in the middle of the night."

"As I said, to refresh everyone's memories about procedures. Your job, all of you," he circled his finger at the group, "is to keep the passengers calm as you move them to the safety of the interior of the ship."

"Do you want to run a drill with them?" Joan asked.

Her father shook his head. "No, that would only increase anxiety already raised at dinner last night. If anything should happen, I'll announce an alert and you all will see everyone gets where they need to be. All right? Just be aware." He dismissed them.

People stood and wearily replaced the chairs around the tables.

"What time is it?" Brylie asked Monica.

"Time to go back to bed." Monica brushed her hair back from her face and sent a smile over Brylie's shoulder.

Brylie turned to see Marcus smiling back.

"It's a little after four," he offered.

She gave a brief nod of thanks and faced her friend. "I'm going to actually get some things going in the kitchen. Kristen will be down before long to get breakfast going."

"Do what you want, I'm going to bed." Monica followed the others who were clearing out.

"I'll give you a hand," Marcus said from behind her.

"I don't need one." Bad enough he'd insisted on sitting beside her in the meeting, though that had been painless enough. The last thing she needed was him trailing after her into the place she considered her sanctuary.

"Sure you do." He followed her through the swinging door. "I won't be able to sleep now anyway."

She could hardly fault him for that, since that was the reason she decided to stay. "It's not going to happen, you know. In the cruises I've been on, we've only seen another ship twice once we passed New Zealand."

He folded his arms. "That makes it a little scarier, if you ask me."

"Maybe." She didn't want to think about it, and didn't want to admit that Marcus being in here with her made her feel just a touch more secure. She couldn't say why that was. She pulled down the flour and crossed to the refrigerator for eggs.

"What are you making?"

"I'm going to start with a coffee cake."

"I thought you weren't the baker."

"I'm not, but I've got a taste for it. And if I can't bake something in my own kitchen…"

He braced his hands on the counter behind him. "Give me something to do."

She took a deep breath, trying to think what she could assign him to keep him busy—and as far from her as the kitchen allowed. Any other time, she would be able to find dozens of things to do in here, but he scrambled her brain. She wouldn't be able to think straight until he left. She hated that weakness. "Have you ever been in a kitchen before?"

"I have, actually. But not since I was six. We had a cook, Miss Elizabeth. I'd spend most every weekend morning with her, making pancakes and biscuits."

She shook her head as she measured out the flour and sifted it into a bowl. The picture of a young Marcus came to her, too easily. She had to push that kind of sentimentality away. It was too early in the cruise to let him get under her skin. "But not in the past couple of decades?"

"I found other people to pester after her. But she taught me a lot. I can flip a mean pancake. Just point me to a skillet."

***

Even at the age of six, he'd managed to make the dishes Brylie instructed him to create, step by step, as if she didn't expect much of him. Well, that made her about on par with the rest of his family, now, didn't it? But the tension eased from her face and shoulders as she bossed him around, so he put up with it, sliding the coffee cake in the oven, fetching eggs from the giant refrigerator so he could make the pancakes, while she made syrup—homemade syrup—on the stove.

She nodded her approval at the pancakes, then inclined her head toward the industrial coffee maker on the other counter. "Do you know how to make coffee?"

He didn't want to admit that the machine intimidated him, that what he knew about coffee could fit in a recyclable paper cup, so he crossed to inspect it. Okay. More moving parts than he was willing to risk screwing up. Just what he needed—three weeks on a ship with caffeine-deprived passengers.

"Does it have instructions?"

She set her whisk beside the pot. "Here, you stir this, I'll do that. Don't stop stirring or it will burn, got it?"

He backed away from the coffee maker, hands raised in surrender. "Yes, ma'am."

He took up the whisk, but didn't take his gaze from her. She was incredible, moving from one task to another fluidly, in constant motion. She crossed to take the pot from him, poured the thickened syrup into two containers and wiped off the liquid that had dripped down the side.

"Now you can make the orange juice." She pointed to a bowl of oranges and a knife down the counter.

"I think you like bossing me around," he observed, flipping the knife off the counter and catching it by the handle. A control thing, he figured. A little too much like his brother Harris, but at least she looked good doing it.

She flashed him a grin. "There is some satisfaction in it."

He paused. "The satisfaction will come later. I guarantee it."

He was rewarded by her blush before he turned his attention to the oranges. "The coffee cake smells amazing."

She crossed to the oven and checked on it, taking a deep breath as she did.

"I hope it's done before everyone else gets here. I don't want to share."

"Except with me?"

She considered him a moment, then straightened. "I suppose you've earned it."

And it was worth every order, from the cinnamon and sugar crumble to the moist yellow cake swirled with more cinnamon. He closed his eyes in appreciation as the cake melted in his mouth, then opened them to see Brylie grinning.

"Best coffee cake ever, right?"

"Best I've ever had."

"It's funny." She swirled her fork over her own piece. "I prefer cooking to baking, unless it's a comfort thing. My grandmother was a baker and owned her own bakery. When I'd stay with her, I'd wake up early and help her. This is her recipe."

"She must have made a fortune." He took another bite.

Brylie sighed. "That wasn't important to her. Independence was."

"So was she?"

Brylie sipped her coffee and nodded. "To the very last day of her life."

"I suppose you take after her, then?"

A corner of her mouth lifted in affirmation as she set the cup down carefully. "You? Do you take after anyone?"

"I do my level best not to." He sat back, turning the handle of his coffee cup in the other direction. "Though I suppose my grandfather was a bit of a hell-raiser in the day."

"Is he why you're here?"

"No, he's dead. He's why you're here, though. He started this whole thing." He waved his hand to encompass the ship. "I mean, we were always wealthy, but he made us over the top, you know? Top five percent or something. Meanest man you'd ever meet, and I loved him with everything in me. He was smart, he was determined, and he died before he saw his dreams come true." He grinned. "So yeah, the temper is the only thing I take from him."

"Like the guy you punched in the nose."

He blinked. "I told you about that?" It wasn't exactly something he was proud of.

"You mentioned it."

His lips twitched and he focused on his coffee cup. "Clearly I wasn't trying too hard to impress you with my machismo."

"Clearly," she echoed, but her tone was playful, more like the girl he'd met in Hobart than the ice queen he'd followed around on the ship.

"There were extenuating circumstances."

"You told me he was an asshole."

"Right, but that's not exactly extenuating. I'm not that big of a dick." She had to be thinking of him as a hot-tempered, hard-partying man-whore. The need to make her understand was overwhelming—and unnerving. When was the last time he cared what someone thought of his actions? He curved his hands around his cup and met her gaze. "My mate, a good friend, died of an overdose that week. He'd been having trouble, you know, adjusting after he stopped competing. Kind of hard to come to grips with his death, since hell, we'd been partying together just the week before. Both of us had more money than sense. That day, the day of the fight, was his funeral. When I got arrested, my family figured they needed to intervene. They gave me a couple of choices. This is the one I took. I figure I need something to occupy me so I don't end up like Jon. This might be the thing."

She was quiet for a moment. "I can't imagine not knowing what you're going to do next. I always know. But I have to say, I don't see you as a corporate man."

He choked out a laugh. "Definitely not."

"A troubleshooter, maybe, someone who goes on the cruises and sees what can be improved."

His mouth turned down. "I don't see that, either. I'm not very social."

"You've done fine here."

He waved a hand, snorting a laugh. "No tuxes or any of that other garbage required. I've pretty much just been myself."

"You can be yourself in a tux."

He laughed again. "No. I can't."

Brylie jolted when the dining room door swung open. Marcus looked over his shoulder to see one of the women from her staff enter. Brylie gathered up the dishes with a bit more haste than he deemed necessary, almost like she didn't want anyone to see her relaxing.

"Time to get back to work. I'll see you later."

So he'd been dismissed. Fine. He could live with that—for now.

"Marcus!" she called when he'd reached the doorway to the dining room.

He turned.

"I'm sorry about your friend. Really."

Her words surprised him. In all the hullabaloo after the fight, no one had said anything about Jon. He nodded his appreciation and left.

***

Brylie jolted when she walked out of the kitchen that night to see Marcus sitting at one of the tables in the darkened dining room. Joe and Peter still bused tables on the far side of the room, and some of her staff remained in the kitchen cleaning up, but her part of the day was done. Marcus rose when she stopped in the doorway.

"Did you sit down at all today?" he asked.

"For a bit. After the lunch rush." She lifted a bottle of water to her lips.

He moved forward and took the bottle from her. "Then you need something stronger than that."

Brylie frowned as she met his gaze, and he inclined his head toward the wine storage in the kitchen behind her.

She straightened. "We can't."

"I'm the owner, right?" He walked through the door to the storage, ignoring the kitchen staff who watched him warily. He looked over his shoulder at Brylie, waiting.

"I'm pretty sure that's not why you're here. It's like raiding your parents' liquor cabinet."

"Aw, come on. You can call my brother for permission if it makes you feel better."

Brylie hesitated, tempted. She would love the ease a good glass of wine would bring, but last time she had something to drink, well, she'd ended up in Marcus's bed. And frankly, that outcome was looking way too attractive again. Maybe it was the relentless testosterone rolling off him, the wiseass remarks he was making, or just the fact that he'd spent time with her today and was waiting for her now. Yeah, her defenses were way down.

She crossed to the keypad and edged him out of the way with her shoulder. "I'll do it."

"Don't trust me?" he asked, curving his body around hers as she attempted to hide the keypad from him as she typed in the numbers.

His breath was hot on her neck, his body hard against her back, and she wanted to lean back into his strength, his heat, his steadiness. She wanted to feel his lips on her skin. But her staff was nearby and no doubt curious. Damn Marcus for being so persistent and getting his way.

"Nope," she said instead, and opened the closet.

He slipped past her to eye the racks of bottles before decisively selecting one and turning to go.

"Aren't you going to ask if I like it?" she asked.

"You will," he said, and closed the door.

Of all the arrogant—but she still followed him as he snagged two glasses and a corkscrew and headed back toward the dining room. She trailed after him.

He didn't stop there, but she did. "I'm not going with you to your room."

"Nope. The lounge."

That, she could go along with. No doubt there would be people around enjoying the moonlight on the waves. She'd be saved from her own bad impulses. She followed him up the stairs, weaving a bit when the ship rolled beneath her. He gripped her elbow to steady her, and they entered the lounge, which was empty. Huh. It must be later than she thought.

"How long were you waiting for me?"

"Too long." He pointed to two chairs amidship, facing the windows. "There."

When she sat, he handed her the glasses and uncorked the wine with an elegance that showed his competence. He poured the red evenly into the glasses and handed her one, steadying the bottle between his feet when he sat. He watched her face as she sipped, and she closed her eyes to avoid his gaze as the deep fruity flavor burst on her tongue.

"You like it?"

"Mm. Very smooth."

"My family's shiraz. My very favorite."

She opened her eyes and looked at him. The dark lounge made this feel too intimate. If she knew what was good for her, she'd get up and leave. "Is there anything your family doesn't have their fingers in?"

He grinned as if he had a dirty joke on the tip of his tongue, but instead of sharing, he settled in the low-backed chair and sipped. "This is my sister's baby, the winery. My brother runs the ships."

"And you snowboard."

He tipped his wine glass toward her. "Hey, I've made some money off that, the endorsements and the equipment companies who sponsored me. If I'd competed another year, I'd have had even more."

She lifted her glass to her lips, watching him. "But you didn't want to."

"Nope."

"What about working with your sister in the winery?"

"It's in one place. Not sure I could do that. Stay in one place, I mean."

"That's a pretty bold statement, don't you think?" Especially for a man trying to get into a woman's good graces.

He shrugged. "I've got itchy feet, which is why my brother Harris thought this might be the place for me."

"So what did you do today while I was slaving away making your kitchen one of the best in the fleet?"

He rolled his eyes. "Watched a lot of waves. Talked to the little girl, Trinity, in the presence of her family. Tried to avoid your father."

She swirled the wine in her glass, smiling despite herself. "Why?"

"Hard to spend time with a man when all you can think about is making love to his daughter."

A flash of warmth shot through her at his words, but she shifted her knees away. She took a drink as flashes of memories from the other night filled her mind. She toed off her shoes and pushed them under her chair, determined he would not see her squirm. "Did the passengers have any idea about the pirate alert?"

He sat back, taking her cue. "If they did, they didn't say anything. They're all excited because they want to ride the zodiac around the icebergs. Not for a couple of days, though, Josh said."

"We won't see icebergs for a few miles," she confirmed. "But they might get the zodiac out tomorrow if we stay on schedule. Did you see any whales today?"

"I didn't. They may have."

"The first few days aren't too exciting, which is why we have the scientists on board giving lectures and showing videos."

He rolled his eyes. "I'm sure it's very interesting and all, but I don't sit still very well. If I hadn't thought you'd bite my head off, I would've come back in to the kitchen."

"Why would you think I'd bite your head off?"

He gave her a look.

"You're my boss," she reminded him.

"Because that's stopped you from tearing into me before."

"I haven't—"

Another look.

She set her glass on the table between them and folded her hands in front of her contritely. "Okay, I haven't been very nice. I'm sorry."

"I get it." He added a bit more wine. "Putting distance. And I haven't made it easy."

"It's okay." She saluted him with her glass. "You're not so bad."

"I appreciate that." He grinned and settled back. "So your dad's here, and you've told me about your grandmother. What about your mother?"

Brylie curled her toes in her thick socks, focusing on the waves illuminated by the ship's running lights. "She left when I was young. Had her own thing to do, didn't want to sit around waiting for my dad."

"She left you behind?"

She winced at his incredulous tone. The last things she wanted was for him to feel sorry for her. She'd spent plenty of time doing that for herself before she'd shaken herself out of it and moved forward. "Yeah, but I'm over it." She crept her feet up the cool glass of the window. "What about you? You have a brother and a sister. What about your parents?"

He lifted a nonchalant shoulder. "They're around, try to be a bit more involved than the three of us would like, I think. Of course, with me, they're thinking it's a preventive measure."

"You don't think of rich parents as being involved. You think nannies, boarding schools—"

"Oh, we had plenty of both. I think when I got kicked out of the third boarding school, they figured they'd better start paying attention. That was when I got into snowboarding. The therapist thought I needed an outlet for my temper." He rolled his eyes at the phrasing.

She shifted to look at him, her legs back on the chair, knees against the armrest. "See, that's what I don't get. I haven't seen one sign that you're short tempered. You were definitely out of your element today, but very patient."

He leaned toward her as if imparting a secret. She bent her head and felt the wash of his breath on her cheek as he said, "That's because I'm trying to seduce you."

She laughed despite herself. Amazing that he would open up to her like this, even if he was only trying to lure her back to his bed. She couldn't remember the last time a man had been honest with her to do so.

He eased back, giving her a measuring look. "So what's on the agenda tomorrow?"

"We may reach the Auckland Islands tomorrow, and they'll take the zodiacs out. There's a big sea lion community there. You'd like going on the zodiac, I'd imagine."

"Do you go?"

"I'm working."

"You have a crew. Can't you leave them alone for a couple of hours? Or are you using the kitchen to avoid me?"

Again she had to resist the urge to fidget. "I'm not."

"Then come on the zodiac with me tomorrow." He stroked a knuckle down her cheek.

The sensation vibrated from his touch down to her nipples and she used every ounce of will not to let her eyelids flutter shut, to let the moan escape her lips. "I've never been on the zodiac."

"Never?"

She shook her head and took a sip of wine, breaking contact with his touch.

"Then I insist."

And just as she envisioned boarding the low-sided rubber boat and skimming across the waves, watching him grin, hear him laugh, he leaned in and kissed her, a long, deep kiss flavored with wine. Her first instinct was to pull away, but instead she curved her hand around the back of his head and she kissed him back.

"You want to get out of here?" he asked finally.

She unfolded her legs, under no illusion about what he meant, wondering at her own willingness to go along. At just what point had she known how this day was going to end? When he'd joined her in the kitchen? Or when she'd walked out to see him waiting for her? "Sure."

He poured the last of the bottle into each of their glasses, then took her elbow to guide her toward the hallway. "Your cabin's closer, I think."

She understood that he wanted to be able to slip free afterwards, was almost relieved by the knowledge that he would leave, and she could regain her sanity for the rest of the cruise. So she led the way to her room, opening it with her keycard though her hand was shaking with the decision she'd made. He stood close, his hand on the small of her back, his head bent so that his breath rushed over her throat. She wouldn't blame alcohol or loneliness this time. She'd made the choice because she wanted him. She opened the door and brought him inside.

He tucked the wine glasses in the cup holders on her private table, then turned to her, curving his hands over her hips. He crowded her against the wall as he brought his mouth down on hers, his lips firm and dry, his breath flavored with the shiraz. She quivered, waiting for the kiss to deepen. Instead, he brushed his mouth back and forth over her parted lips, then dipped his tongue between them. A needy sound tore from her throat as she slipped her hands up his arms to his shoulders—so hard—before curling around the back of his neck, her fingers playing over the short hair there. She angled her head to deepen the kiss as she pulled him closer. He chuckled against her mouth and drew her hips forward, so she could feel his arousal. Memories of the other night, of how he felt against her, inside her, flooded her with desire. She slid her hands down his back, ducked her hands under his arms to slip under his sweatshirt, over his firm, warm skin.

Shuffling a step forward, he pinned her to the wall with his hips, his thigh between hers, then leaned back enough to strip the sweatshirt and his T-shirt off. He tossed it over a nearby chair and reached for the hem of her top. Wanting to feel his chest hair against her skin, she wriggled out of the garment and leaned forward. He smoothed his hands down her back to her hips and dipped his head to kiss her again, his lips more demanding now. She pressed her breasts against his chest, her nipples hard through the lace of her bra.

He muttered something about her being a surprising librarian and slipped his hands between them to unfasten her jeans before reaching inside.

She cried out and dropped her head back at his intimate touch, then clutched at his shoulders to put some space between them. "Not yet. Not yet, Marcus."

He lifted his head, breathing heavily. "I don't have much control just now, Brylie."

"Fine." She shed her jeans and stood before him in her lace underwear and bra. "But I hope you have a condom."

His gaze swept over her, hot and hungry, and he made a strangled sound. She slipped past him to the bed, not quite queen-sized. She laid back, one leg bent, and he dropped himself over her, bracing his weight on his arms. He kissed her again, this one almost sloppy with need. His forehead rubbed against hers as she slid her bare legs along his jean-clad ones.

"You don't pack in case of emergency?" he asked.

"We used mine last time." She skimmed her hand over the front of his jeans and he groaned. "Don't tease me here, Marcus."

He lifted his head and grinned, holding up his wallet. To her relief, he drew out a condom, and she noticed he had a spare. Thank God.

He rose off her long enough to shuck his jeans and shorts, then covered her again, kissing her mouth, moving to her jaw, finding the sensitive spot below her ear. His chest hair caught in the lace of her bra and that small sensation sent another tremor of lust through her. She slid her fingers from his belly over his chest, fingers flexing in the crisp hair, before she cupped his head in her hands and pulled him down to kiss her. Her hips lifted into his, an unmistakable invitation. He hooked his fingers in her underwear and pulled them down. The delicate fabric tore and she winced.

"Sorry. Christ."

When he glided his hands up the backs of her legs, all was forgiven. He lifted his head to look into her eyes as he pushed inside of her.

So much better this time, when she could zero in on every sensation, his weight on her, the flex of his muscles, the play of his mouth on her skin. They found a rhythm that was accented by the pitch of the ship, and Brylie alternately laughed in delight and groaned in pleasure.

Gripping her hips, he rolled with her, still deep inside, so that he was on his back and she was over him. He loosened her bra, freeing her breasts, and lifted his head to capture a nipple between his lips, rolling it with his tongue. Her fingers curling in his hair, she cried out, holding him to her as she rode him. He palmed her bottom, adjusting her, parting her, and they drove into each other until her legs burned and her body was tight with the need for release.

He gave it to her with a swipe of his finger, then tilted her onto her back to find his own.

Quivering, her hands skimmed down his sweaty back as his breath gusted against her throat. He flopped onto his back. When she chanced a look at him, he gave her a grin that would take her breath away if she had any left.

"We are really good at this." He twisted to kiss her and sat up in the same movement, climbing off the bed. "Do you have your own bathroom?"

"Through there."

He bent to give her another, lingering kiss before disappearing in the attached room. He returned a moment later and crawled back in bed, sliding his legs between the flannel sheets, under the thermal blankets.

"You prefer a side?" he asked, his back to the bulkhead as he leaned on his elbow.

She couldn't think of what to say. She'd expected he'd stay maybe a few minutes more, then bolt back to his room. She didn't think he'd make himself at home in her bed.

"I—don't care. You don't have to stay."

He folded his hands behind his head. "You want me to go?"

"No. You don't need to go." The idea of sleeping in his arms sent twin shivers of terror and longing through her.

"Good. I'm comfortable here." He hooked his arm around her waist and drew her beneath the covers, her back against his chest. He smoothed his hand over her hair and settled his head against her pillow.

***

Marcus woke with a start. Sunlight streamed through the shuttered windows onto the bed. Brylie's cloud of red hair snagged in his stubble. She smelled delicious, some kind of fruity shampoo or something, mingled in with her own scent. His arousal nudged at her bottom and she made a soft sound of approval in her sleep. He shifted, careful not to disturb her, and rubbed his eyes. Something had woken him, and it wasn't his inner alarm telling him to get out of a woman's bed. He wondered where that alarm was.

Instead, he listened to an unfamiliar hum vibrating in the air.

"Brylie." He rubbed his hand up and down her arm to wake her. "What's that sound?"

"Hm?" She woke slowly, turned toward him before she opened her eyes dreamily. "Hey. You're still here."

"What's that sound?" he asked again. "It's different. Like an engine." He hadn't heard the engine of the Ice Queen since he'd been on board—that was supposed to be part of the excellence of the ship.

She lifted her head when shouting outside her window carried over the other sound. He sat up then and peered through the slats of the porthole shutters. What he saw had his heart arresting before pumping adrenaline through his body. Another ship had pulled alongside the Ice Queen, about a third of the size, and men were on deck, waving their arms as black smoke poured from the chimney. Brylie pressed her face close, to look, too.

"Are they in trouble?" he asked, though some instinct told him they weren't. He strained to see the security team Captain Winston had spoken of, but couldn't from this angle. Surely they'd move into position since they were under an alert.

She shifted away from him. "We should go see what's going on."

And then, while Marcus watched, Brylie's father approached. Marcus's skin iced when the men on the other ship pulled out automatic weapons.

CHAPTER THREE

Marcus rolled into action, pushing Brylie off the bed ahead of him. "Get dressed. Quickly. In something warm."

He bent to snatch up his clothes as the sound of machine gun fire rang out. Brylie made a sound of distress and lunged for the window, but Marcus grabbed her. The last thing he wanted her to see was her father bleeding on the deck. He gripped her shoulders and looked into her face.

"Brylie. Think. Where can we hide?"

"The closet? The bathroom? I don't know!"

They'd be trapped in those places. He released her with another curt order to get dressed, and scanned the room, and the ceiling. Solid. Hell. He opened the door into the hallway and saw what he was looking for, tiles that could be pushed up and likely had a crawlspace. The trick was getting up there, and quickly. He hoped it would hold their weight. He turned back into the room to see Brylie pulling on a thermal shirt over those gorgeous breasts.

"Warm, do you understand me?" he said again, reaching for his boxers and jeans, tangled together at the edge of the bed.

She pulled on a sweater, then another sweatshirt as he dressed, two pair of socks, and dug a pair of gloves out as he laced up his boots.

"Any ID, bring it with you."

She gave him a puzzled look but opened a drawer and tucked cards into her jeans pocket. One of the cards was blank, with a black strip along the back.

"What's that?" he asked.

"My master key card. In case."

He nodded. Good thinking. "Ready?"

She nodded. "Are you sure—?"

"Best to hide and figure it out later, yeah? We're going in the hall and I'm going to give you a boost. Be careful not to put your weight directly on the tiles or you'll fall through, okay?"

"Marcus." Her face was pale in the dim light, her eyes dark with fear. "I can't. The passengers. We have to get them to safety. You know what my father said."

He hesitated. Every molecule in his body, that he'd trained himself to listen to, told him to bolt, to hide. But she was right. The passengers were his responsibility.

"I'll go." He couldn't allow her to come up her father's bleeding body on the deck. He couldn't be sure the man had been shot, but he'd been bloody close to the terrorists. Damn, he wished he knew what was going on, if the security guys had gone into action with those power hoses—and if that had been effective.

"I have to go. My father—"

Gunfire below them cut her off. Automatic weapons fired in staccato bursts, and hand guns popped. *Ours or theirs?* Screams from the passengers. Marcus realized getting all the passengers to the interior of the ship, in one place, would make it easier for the terrorists to hurt them. No. He and Brylie had to find a way to hide, to call for help.

"We won't be able to get to them without getting caught ourselves." He flinched when another gunshot went off, this one closer, from what sounded like the stairwell. He jumped up and hit the ceiling tile with the tips of his fingers to make sure it moved. When it shifted to his satisfaction, he turned to Brylie, who was wild-eyed and tense enough to snap.

He placed a hand on her shoulder to focus her. "Trust me."

He went down on a knee, forming a cup with his hand and she placed her booted foot into it. Straining, he lifted her until she could reach the ceiling. She shoved a tile out of her way and pulled herself through as he rose, pushing her along.

"Good girl," he muttered.

More shouting from the deck had him hesitate. She was safe, but did he have time to follow her up, or would he get caught and give her away? He scanned her room for a quick way to give him a boost, but using something like that would leave a clue about where they'd gone. He closed her bedroom door and looked up into her face as she leaned down to help him.

He grasped her wrists, and with his foot on the railing on the other side of the hallway, he pushed himself up and into the crawlspace beside her. He got the paneling in place just as he heard footsteps in the hall. He cradled Brylie against him, feeling her shivering, as a loud crash sounded down the hall, then another.

They were kicking in doors, looking for passengers.

What the hell did they want?

He dragged Brylie closer, against the wall, making sure her weight was braced on the metal supports and not on the tile where the ceiling would sag, giving them away. He ran a soothing hand over her hair, though his own heart was pounding like hell. Because he couldn't risk shushing her, he pressed his lips to her forehead, hoping she'd get the message.

She did, only quivering as the footsteps approached, then jumping as the door right below them—her door— was kicked in. As he watched, her foot slipped off the metal support, but she caught herself millimeters from letting her heel hit the tile above the heads of the men below.

Carefully she set it on the support, and they remained still as they listened to the men move down the hall.

Marcus didn't know how long they waited. His leg muscles ached with holding still, with holding his balance on the metal. His arms ached with holding Brylie, so afraid she'd slip. He heard nothing below them, and only after several moments did he dare look through the tiles into the hallway.

"Clear," he said, so close to her ear as to not make a sound. But he didn't dare reenter the main walkway. No, they'd have to see how much progress they could make in the crawlspace.

"The radio," she whispered.

He nodded once, then pointed in all directions and shrugged. *Which way?* She took a deep breath and inclined her head to the right, then got on her hands and knees and started that direction, careful to keep her weight on the struts, moving slowly, her movements unsteady as the edges pressed into her flesh.

They reached a wall. She stopped and rocked back a little, rubbing her forehead, which creased in thought. He tapped her shoulder and pointed to a panel to their left. Pressing both hands against it, he lifted it up, wincing as it scraped, pausing before a moment before deciding it had to be done.

The passageway he revealed was narrower, and this time he led the way, since there didn't seem to be many options anyway. He started through, and heard Brylie's sharp breath behind him. He twisted to see her, pale and drawn, and hesitating.

He tried to reach back to her, to encourage her, but there wasn't room. He had to hope this tunnel opened up somewhere, somewhere safe. And he had to hope when he moved forward, Brylie would follow. He didn't know what else to do. So he started crawling, listening for noise behind him, and below. He finally heard her breath behind him, shaky, but behind him. He grinned. Yeah, she was tougher than she thought. Good for her.

He found another panel like the one they'd come through. Please God let it be a bigger passageway, or maybe just a place where they could stop and think. He didn't know if there was a place on the ship like that. They needed to be able to catch their breath, and he needed a drink. Water would be good, too.

She gripped his arm and drew him down another, smaller passageway, though he hadn't thought *that* was possible. Warmth flowed toward them, then the passageway opened up and Brylie sat against a wall, drawing in deep breaths.

"We can talk here," she said above a mechanical hum. The surface beneath them was solid and warm.

"Where are we?" He shifted his weight to sit next to her. He didn't know their location in relation to the bad guys, and they couldn't risk being overheard.

She let her head fall back against the wall. "On top of my freezer."

He hadn't expected that. He looked around, but they were boxed in, only the vent wall open. "What? The kitchen? How do you know?"

"Because we're on top of my freezer," she said slowly, as if to a child. "Where else would a freezer be?"

"Wouldn't there be a fan or coils or something?"

"All on the inside. We're closed in here, safe. No one should be able to find it."

"How did you know this was here?"

"I saw this space when they were installing it. I asked why it was here. The guys said it needed space to vent the heat."

He shifted on the warm appliance. Yeah, he could see that.

"So what do we do next?" she asked.

He dragged a hand over his face. Why did she think he had any answers? "The radio. We have to get to the radio and let someone know what's going on."

She pressed her lips together as if considering it.

"You have another idea?"

"I'm thinking about getting some food."

"We can eat later."

"I mean to save. If they're here to wipe out our supplies, it's a long journey back without food."

"You think they're here to raid the ship?" He hadn't considered that option, not once he'd seen the guns. What he'd thought—well, he hadn't. He'd just acted.

"Why do you think they're here?"

He shook his head. "They're looking for someone." Or everyone.

"Maybe you?"

He looked at her sharply. That hadn't occurred to him, but he was the owner—one of them, anyway. And his family was one of the wealthiest families in the world. That people would be after him wasn't outside the realm of possibility. In fact, it had been one of his mother's fears for years, especially when he'd eschewed precautions to pursue an Olympic medal. "I should go out there, then."

She shot forward and gripped his arm, her eyes wide. "Are you crazy? You heard those guns. You don't know what they'll do to you."

He shook his head, careful not to dislodge her hand. Witnessing her fright was unnerving. "I don't know what they'll do to the others. I'm responsible." Christ, did that sound odd coming out of his mouth. The feeling that accompanied the words was even odder. He'd never been responsible for another soul in his life.

She curved her hand on his wrist. "We need to see what they want. Maybe they're just here to raid, and if so, let them take what they want and go. Maybe they don't even know you're here. Don't be rash."

He scrubbed his hand over his mouth. His impulse was to get to the radio, so help could be on its way, whether or not the men stayed. "We need to get to the bridge and call for help. Can we get to the bridge through this crawlspace?"

She shook her head. "It's a different level. We're going to have to move through some hallways."

The idea of being in the open made his skin crawl. If these men were truly pirates, what were they capable of? His stomach clenched at the idea of them getting their hands on Brylie.

He thought of Trinity, the pretty little blonde teenager, and the other women on board who were vulnerable. Christ. "We need to find out why they're here, and hope to God they don't stay long." But he had a bad feeling that hope wouldn't come true.

He almost wished he'd been able to observe them a bit longer, see what went down on the deck. That would give him more insight about what the men on the other ship wanted. But if he and Brylie hadn't moved as quickly as they did, they'd be prisoners. Or worse.

Damn, he hated not knowing what was going on. He rubbed the back of his neck.

"I'll stay and get the food. You go to the bridge," she suggested.

"I'm not leaving you here alone. Five minutes, Brylie. No more. All right?"

***

Brylie's heart pounded as she kept watch on the door between the dining room and kitchen while Marcus grabbed cases of bottled water and prepackaged food. They'd removed one of the freezer's fans to get into the freezer, then the kitchen, using his pocketknife to remove the screws on the appliance. She'd wanted to be the one to collect the food since she knew where everything was. For awhile, he'd allowed it and kept watch for her, but she hadn't moved quickly enough for him. He'd convinced her that he was able to lift more, and quicker, than she was.

A hand rested on her upper arm and she jumped, barely smothering a squeal as she spun and looked into Marcus's eyes.

"Time to go."

She could barely nod her understanding, her nerves were so scattered after his silent approach. "Did you get everything?" she stuttered at last.

He nodded. "Everything you showed me. Now. How do I get to the bridge from here?"

She wished they could have a moment to recover. She was not cut out for crises. She had planned everything out for this trip. She'd thought Marcus would be her biggest distraction. Now she wished he was.

Her stomach was in knots wondering what her father was dealing with, if he was okay. She'd heard the gunshots that had propelled Marcus out of bed. Had her father been the target? Was he still alive?

But Marcus was waiting for her to tell him how to get to the bridge. He needed her. And she needed to find out what had happened to her father.

She took the hand Marcus held out and led the way back into the freezer. She wished she knew the ship better, that they would be able to move without risking being seen. Her plan was to travel from the kitchen through the crawlway to the stairs. Once they got to the level with the bridge, well, she wasn't sure how far the crawlspace went, if it was like this level or different. She didn't want to be caught out in the open. No telling what would happen to them if they were found, no telling what would happen to Marcus especially, if the intruders learned he was one of the owners of this ship.

***

The crawlspace was much like the one on the lower level, but it ended before they reached the bridge. All this sneaking around made Marcus fidgety. If it was up to him, he'd charge down the hall to the bridge and make the call, damn whoever might be between him and the radio. But that action would leave Brylie by herself. Why should she pay for his impulsiveness? She'd be scared and alone, and while he wasn't the best protector, he was better than nothing. He'd never had anyone to look out for before. He wasn't so sure he liked it. It made him second-guess everything.

With Brylie on his heels, he pulled aside the panel and checked out the hallway. Empty. Voices sounded from behind the door of the bridge. He didn't know who was in there, but he didn't think it was Brylie's father. The voices were heavily accented so he couldn't tell if they whether or not they were speaking English. Shit. They were too late. The bridge was occupied. To be fair, though, they probably would have been too late even if they hadn't stopped in the kitchen. Hell, if he was a pirate, the first thing he'd do was take over the bridge and the communications. Shit, shit, shit. He sat up and pulled the panel back into place, resting his head against the wall, not meeting Brylie's gaze.

"Is it clear?" she asked, her lips barely moving.

He shook his head. "Don't know who's in there. Is there a way we can listen in?"

She pushed loose strands of hair back from her face with stiff, impatient movements. "Do you think I designed this ship? I'm the chef."

He gritted his teeth. Just what they needed, to take their frustration out on each other. He squeezed her shin, scanning the area. End of the road.

"I'm going to go down and listen at the door."

"No!" The word came out loud enough to vibrate off the wall, and her hand clamped over his. "You'll get caught."

"No, I won't. I'll be careful." This time he drew his hand away, tired of being in the dark, of having to consider someone else when he was used to doing whatever he wanted.

"If they come out, or someone else comes down the hall, where will you go?"

He considered, every muscle in his body quivering with his need to do something, to find out what the hell these people wanted and how bad they wanted it. "Give me your master key card. I'll slip in the room next door."

She pulled the card out of her back pocket and held it out, then pulled it out of his reach. "I'm going with you."

He went rigid. "The hell you are." But he thought about it a moment. He would feel better if she was in his sight. Though he'd hate himself if they got caught and she got hurt, or worse. He gave her a curt nod and turned away, leaving her with the key card.

He moved the panel again. Bracing his hands on the supports, he lowered his body through the opening, and landed in the hallway in a crouch, wincing at the thump. He straightened, looked around, then reached up to help her down. She lowered her legs through the opening, and he caught her around the knees, taking her weight against his chest when she released the ceiling.

"Put the tile in place," he grunted, and she scrambled to do so, balancing it on the tips of her fingers, then she slid down his body and stepped back.

She moved toward the door by the bridge, ready to slide the key card into the slot.

He grabbed her wrist. "How do we know no one is in there?" he asked.

She pulled the card away and stepped back. "We don't."

He took her place and pressed his ear against the door. He heard nothing. Still..."Get ready to run," he told her, plucking the key card from her hand and sliding it home.

The room they entered housed the servers for communication and navigation, and the hum of the machines made it impossible to hear any of the conversation on the bridge, or to communicate with each other any way other than with gestures. Brylie pointed to a vent above them, just a normal vent like you'd see in a house, sharing a wall with the bridge. Marcus climbed up on one of the metal shelves holding the black machinery and heaved himself up. There was a space between the walls, so he couldn't see directly into the bridge, couldn't see how many men were in there, or who they were, but he could hear their voices. Angry voices, loud, and foreign. Portuguese, maybe? What did they speak in Chile? Brazil was Portuguese, he knew that much.

He crouched down to Brylie. "You know languages?"

She shrugged. "A few words here and there. French, mostly. Some Spanish. Why?"

"Come up here and see if you can tell me what language this is."

Moving as lightly as he could, he hopped off the shelf and helped her take his place. She leaned close against the wall, trying as he had to see into the other room. Then she closed her eyes and listened carefully for a few moments, then lowered herself off the shelf, shaking her head.

"I can't be sure. It sounds like Spanish, but the accent is weird. I don't know."

He nodded. "So, from South America?"

"Maybe." Frustration etched lines on her face. "But this isn't doing us any good. We can't find out why they're here if we can't understand them."

"We're here to call for help," he reminded her. "We can still do that."

Her eyes widened. "How? We can't just walk in there. And we don't even know how many are in there."

"A distraction. I'll make one, take off, and you go in there and call."

She was shaking her head before he was done. "No. No way. I can't."

"Sure you can." He rubbed his hand down her arm reassuringly. "I need you to do this, Brylie."

Panic constricted her features, making her eyes appear even bigger. "We'll give ourselves away. Right now they don't know we're here. If we do that, we'll lose the element of surprise."

She was right. Damn it. But was that more important than alerting authorities?

"Right. Right." He lowered himself to the floor and pulled his legs up in front of them, his elbows on his knees and dragged his hands down his face. Now what?

"We should find out where the others are," she said.

He opened his eyes and looked into hers. She was probably right. The idea of crawling through that confined space again tightened his muscles. He wanted just a moment to catch his breath, gather his thoughts, and figure out how he could get to the radio.

Then Trinity's innocent young face flashed in his mind and he had to move, had to do what he could to help her and the others. Hell, he was no hero. What did he think he could do?

***

Marcus wished they could just walk down the hall to their hiding place. Moving through the crawlspace took too long and was too limiting, and he had no idea where they were in relation to the kitchen. He wished they had a map or something. He didn't like depending on Brylie to be in front—she was too vulnerable. But she knew the direction better, so he deferred to her.

She paused in front of a vent that illuminated her face in stripes and held up her hand, then lifted a finger to her lips, her gaze riveted on the other side of the grate. He wanted to see what she was seeing and edged up, but she scowled over her shoulder as he crowded her.

While he couldn't see, he could hear the voices.

"All depends on you," a man said in heavily accented English. "As long as you follow instructions, it will go easy on you."

"What do you want?" Was that the captain's voice? Relief weakened Marcus's muscles. He hadn't been gunned down on the deck. He reached for Brylie's hand and squeezed. She squeezed back.

"We've contacted Devlin Excursions for ransom."

Marcus heard the murmurs roll through the room before one man—he'd bet the asshole from his table last night, the one worried about the pirates in the first place—spoke up.

"How do you expect them to get the money to you without you being caught?"

"That is not your concern. Your concern is to follow the rules and stay alive."

Finally Brylie must have sensed Marcus's impatience because she edged forward to let him look through the vent. He was able to see a large part of the lounge, where dozens of the passengers sat in the low-backed chairs, wives close to husbands, the group of young adventurers looking defiant, but with fear lining their faces. Marcus had seen that look on rookie snowboarders at the top of the course. He hoped their defiance didn't cause them to do anything stupid. He scanned the room for Trinity but didn't see her, or the captain, either.

He wanted to stay and hear more, but Brylie was slithering down the vent, so he followed. When they were back in the kitchen, on top of the humming freezer, he saw she was crying, and shaking with it. Smart girl, she hadn't wanted anyone to hear them. He wrapped his arms around her and pulled her against his chest, smoothing her hair, murmuring nonsense until she pushed away, turning her head and wiping at her tears with the heel of her hand.

"Was that your dad's voice I heard?"

She nodded, still not looking at him. "I can't believe they have him."

"At least he's safe."

She nodded again, this one jerkier. "I thought they'd killed him."

He didn't know if he should tell her he thought so, too.

"They could still kill him," she said on a shuddering breath.

"We're not going to let that happen."

"How can we stop it?" Her voice lifted in her panic.

He had to calm her. He needed her reasonable, and on his side, though he understood her meltdown and wished he could have one of his own. "I'll find a way."

Brylie shoved her hair back from her face and shook her head. Suddenly, she lifted her face to his, her expression bright, hopeful. "Wait. I think I know where there might be another radio, and it might be easier to get to than the bridge."

His pulse jumped at the possibility. "Where?"

***

The engine room was hot and steamy, the narrow corridors making it difficult for Marcus to keep an eye on Brylie as she followed him. She'd wanted to lead, but this time he couldn't risk it, not when a terrorist could be lurking down here. For a moment, he wondered what would happen if he managed disabled the ship in some way, but that was too drastic a step to take, yet. Who wanted to be stranded in the middle of the Southern Ocean without power? So he kept with the original plan—find a radio, call for help.

How long would it take help to reach them? Right, that was out of his control. Hell, everything here was out of his control. Usually control was an abstract concept for him—he sure didn't have any over his temper. But he always had a piece of his life that he had a grip on. Maybe his home, maybe a girl, maybe his game, maybe his buddies.

Since Jon died, he felt a hell of a lot less in control.

At least they were able to walk down here. His knees and palms were already sore from crawling along metal brackets, and his back ached with the tension of remaining hunched over. He reached back for Brylie's hand. She hesitated, then slid her hand into his. He squeezed, grateful for the contact, and continued down the corridor.

His heart jumped when he saw a phone, but she grabbed his wrist before he picked it up. She pointed at a plastic sign above it. "To the bridge." Right. Wouldn't want to let the baddies know they were hanging around down here.

Frustration tensed his shoulders as they continued, unable to find anything. Then she tugged at his hand and pulled him to the right, where she released his hand and hurried forward. He was about to grab her shoulder to stop her when she lifted two radios and turned to him, grinning.

Not radios, he realized, not what they were after, but walkie-talkies. For a moment he wondered at her excitement, but then he realized the options they had here. She handed him one and tucked the other in the pocket of her sweatshirt.

"If we can get one to my father, we can know what's going on."

"You don't think they'd notice him with a walkie?" He shook his head. "You keep one and I keep one."

She scowled. "You're going to bail, aren't you?"

He had to admit, the idea of having some freedom, of not having to constantly worry about her, had appeal. But he doubted she'd go for him locking her away while he went exploring. "If we get separated, you know. If—one of us needs privacy and gets in trouble."

She nodded and turned away, apparently in search of the real radio.

The noise down here made him nervous. No telling what lurked around the corner. Sure couldn't hear someone coming up on you. And Brylie was making him nuts, because the more anxious she got, the quicker she moved, probably as glad as he was to be able to use her feet. He grabbed her arm and she jumped a foot, barely muffling her cry of alarm. Her eyes were huge when she looked back at him, then she sagged against him. He could feel her heart pounding.

"Sorry," he murmured. "You were getting away from me."

His meaning took a moment to sink in, then she nodded and let him move ahead.

They didn't find a radio, or a sat phone, and returned to the freezer alcove empty-handed.

Brylie felt guilty eating when she didn't think the hostages had been fed, so she merely nibbled the packet of fruit snacks Marcus tossed her way.

"Eat up," he advised. "You're the one that told me we need more calories because it's cold."

"It's not cold here," she muttered stubbornly, hunched against the wall.

But they were safe, and that made her feel more guilty than eating. She would be with the others if she'd been at her post instead of in bed with Marcus. So she had to make sure she did something to help those in the lounge.

Sitting in here was making her antsy, and she could tell it was doing the same to Marcus. He hadn't stayed in the same position for more than two minutes. Yes, it wasn't exactly comfortable up here, but his fidgeting made her uneasy.

"I'm going to see what's going on. Is there any way to get topside from here?"

She widened her eyes. "Topside? You're not dressed to go out."

"I'm not going to be out for long," he said, his tone tight. "And I'm used to the cold. Snowboarder, remember? Look, I just want to have a look at their ship, see if I can get an idea how many there are. I won't be gone long. We have the walkies." He pulled his out, set it to a channel to match hers. "I'll be back."

"Then I'm going to the lounge and see what's going on there." He didn't expect her to just sit here, did he?

He shook his head. "If I get in trouble and need to call you, they'll hear the walkie and you'll get caught. Just—wait here. I won't be long, I promise."

"Wait!"

He turned, impatience lining his face.

"Take this." She shoved the master key card at him. "Just in case."

He took it and nodded. "Good thinking. Thanks." Without waiting for her to give him directions, he disappeared into the vent.

***

Once he'd gotten some distance from her, he got tired of crawling around on his hands and knees. Yeah, he could get caught, but he was smart and he was quick. And he needed to think. Not that Brylie was a distraction, really, but worrying about her—that was out of the ordinary. As long as he was worried about her, he couldn't make decisions.

Glancing around the corridor, he headed toward the door that led onto the deck on the third level. He exited on the opposite side from the other ship, afraid someone was watching from the pirates' vessel and would see his movement. That would be bad. He slipped out, and the wind from the ocean almost stole his breath. Brylie was right. He wasn't dressed for this. But he was going nuts locked up in there. He wedged the door open and kept it from closing again with a fire extinguisher. Then he crept along the edge of the ship—Jesus, it was cold—and rounded the corner to look at the other craft.

It was a third of the length of the Ice Queen, but an icebreaker as well, outfitted to go in any direction once they got away. He didn't see anyone on board, but they might be more conscious of the cold. He should have tried to get to his own cabin for his gear before he came out here. He'd do so on the way back. He'd told Brylie to dress warm but didn't remember to get her coat. He'd have to find a way to do that, too. No telling what measures they'd have to take to stay ahead of the pirates, and it was best to be prepared for anything.

He couldn't see a damn thing up here, but dared not get closer. He'd really hoped to learn how many men were on that ship, how many men he had to worry about. He cast a glance up at the helicopter pad, with the sightseeing helicopter, wishing he knew how to fly the thing, how to get help. Instead, he had to get back to Brylie.

***

He was gone too long. Brylie couldn't stand not knowing where he was, couldn't stand waiting. She hooked her walkie onto the waistband of her sweatpants, turned the volume down—no sense in getting caught if Marcus decided to bellow for her—and wished she had paper to leave him a note. She had to go back to the lounge, to see what was going on in there. If he was going off to be brave and foolish, well, at least she should have news for him when she returned. He would be pissed, but, well, he didn't know her if he thought she was just going to stay put because he told her to.

She entered the crawlspace and made her way in the direction of the lounge, moving carefully, worried about her boot hitting the side of the crawlway, or having to sneeze.

But mostly worried about the others and what they were dealing with.

She reached the vent overlooking the lounge in time to hear one of the women ask for food. She peered through the vent and saw the older woman who had come here on an anniversary trip with her husband, fear etched clearly on her pale face. The fruit snack Brylie had eaten turned over in her stomach with guilt.

"No food yet, not until we get a response."

"I need to have food, my blood sugar is dropping," the woman pressed.

Brylie winced as a man stepped into view, looming over the woman threateningly. For a moment, Brylie thought he was going to hit her. The woman cowered, apparently fearing the same thing.

"I'm diabetic," the woman went on. "Please. I'm not asking for special favors. I could die."

"You take the insulin?"

"It's in my cabin. But if I eat something, just a little bit of cheese or fruit, I can manage without the insulin for a little bit. Please."

"Which of you is the cook?" He whirled on the group, and for a moment, Brylie thought he could see her through the grate.

Brylie's heart seized. Here it came—they would notice she was not among them and start searching. Where was Marcus? Was he safely back in their hiding place? If the terrorists started looking for them, how much longer could they hide?

"I'm the cook," Monica spoke up, and Brylie shifted to see her rise, her shoulders back, her head high. "Shall I bring in food for everyone? No one has had breakfast. I'm sure everyone could use the strength."

The terrorist hesitated. For a moment, Brylie was sure he'd refuse. "You may bring in only what you can carry. One of my men will accompany you, but he will not assist."

Monica's expression slackened in fear as another man toting a big gun stepped up beside her.

"Do not make a mistake. Jorge is very good at his job. It would be a shame to be without a cook for the rest of the voyage."

Brylie watched until Monica was marched out of the room. Thank God no one had mentioned her. She didn't want to be pursued through the ship. The idea had fear icing her veins.

She barely covered a shriek of alarm when Marcus tapped her foot, squeezing into the space with her. His expression was thunderous, brows drawn together, mouth tight, eyes dark with temper. At least he couldn't tear into her now. She didn't want to go back into the kitchen yet because that's where Monica and her guard were heading. So she remained, listening, making room for Marcus, hearing his heavy breathing that told her he was ready to have it out. Too bad.

Once Monica and the guard emerged, Brylie slithered forward through the tunnel. Marcus grabbed her ankle and frowned. She motioned to the woman and to the crawlspace, certain he'd understand.

Whether or not he did, he followed her, his mouth grim. When they reached their hiding place, he pinned her to the wall, eyes flashing.

"I should be out there. I should be with them, with the gun held to my head while I bring food to the hostages. Not Monica. Me."

"Christ, Brylie, you can't have your guilt drive you to do something stupid."

She drew back sharply, bumping her head into the wall.

He eased away and shook his head, blowing his temper out on a breath. "Don't look at me like that, Brylie. You know what I mean. We're not going to be any help to anyone if we get caught, will we?"

"What's the point of us being able to move around if we can't help?" she countered.

"I don't know," he snapped. "But we have to think this through. We can't just rush all over the place. We have to get to the bridge. We have to call for help. I just don't know how."

Marcus lay back on the freezer, fingers laced over his chest and closed his eyes.

"Hard for me to think with you vibrating over there," he muttered, not opening his eyes.

"Sorry I can't be all Zen for you," she retorted. "I'm just thinking it's only a matter of time before they check the manifest and realize we're not down there. They'll tear this place apart looking for us, and once they find us—"

"All the more reason to get in to the radio." He rolled onto his side, propping his head on his hand, his elbow on the freezer. "What about the sightseeing helicopter?"

"I don't know how to fly."

"I'm thinking the radio."

She shook her head. "It needs a key to operate, and Carl always has the keys on him."

"Or the bad guys have them." He blew out a breath. Back to plan A. "I need a weapon."

She widened her eyes. "You're not going to confront them?"

"Can you think of another way? Is there any place your dad might keep a gun on board, other than for the security team? No doubt they've been disarmed by now."

"I'm—" She tucked her hair behind her ear. "My dad might have a handgun in his cabin, but it's too risky. Even if you can get to the cabin, you can't go after those men. They're armed to the teeth and experienced with weapons."

"And they don't know we're here. I have surprise on my side."

She shook her head. "No. I can't let you do this."

He leaned forward and closed his hand over hers. "We don't have a choice."

She let out a shuddering breath. "If they figure out we're here, they'll come looking for us."

He drew a sharp breath through his nose, sitting now. "So we'll need a good place to hide. Any ideas?"

She liked where they were now just fine. It wasn't particularly comfortable, but warm, and the hum of the machinery disguised their conversation. Plus it was easily accessible by the vent, and close to the kitchen. If Monica came back in, Brylie could contact her, if she was careful, and get word to her father that she was safe.

She went through the ship's layout in her mind, deck by deck and shook her head. "I can't think of any place more secure."

He pressed his lips together. "I want to be able to hear them coming, and we can't with this noise. If they find us up here, we're trapped. I want a place with another way out. Can you think of someplace like that? Maybe even an outside exit?"

"Dry goods storage, maybe. It's cold in there, though, and we can't be sure they won't be going in there for supplies."

"Two exits?"

She nodded.

"We'll go there, then, but first we'll get our coats. Storage means shelves, I assume. We'll go up high. Should be plenty of stuff to hide behind this early on in the trip."

She nodded.

"Right." He sat on his haunches, hands folded between his knees. "So all we need now is the gun."

***

Marcus waited in the room outside the bridge, where he and Brylie had tried to eavesdrop earlier. He changed his grip on the Glock in his hand, trying to find the right balance. He hadn't been to the range in a few years, and even then, he was only after targets. He didn't know if he could shoot a man. Time to find out.

It had taken them an hour to creep into the captain's room, then back to their own cabins for their coats, every minute excruciating. They had to make the call, but also needed to be prepared if everything went to hell.

He peered into the bridge through the vent, but couldn't see anything, didn't hear any conversation, though the occasional shuffle and roll of a chair let him know someone was in there. He took a deep breath, slipped into the hall, slid the key card into the bridge lock, and entered the code Brylie had shared. He winced when it beeped, then pushed open the door and pressed forward, gun at the ready.

Two men were in the room, one at the controls and one already moving toward him. Marcus brought up the gun but couldn't fire. Instead, he used his arm to block his attacker, swinging his other hand in an upper-cut that connected with the soft belly. He pushed the man back to deliver a more direct hit to the jaw, sending him stumbling.

The man at the controls swung his pistol toward Marcus. Marcus fired wildly, then ducked, driving his shoulder into the man's gut. The pirate fell back into the chair, which skidded across the smooth deck. This time Marcus was off balance. He dropped to his knees a moment before pushing to his feet and shoving the other man's gun straight up. It fired right beside his ear, and he waited for the penetrating pain. Shaking his head to clear the ringing, he gripped the man's wrist and twisted until he heard a snap. The gun clattered to the wooden floor. Marcus snatched it up, pivoting and raising it against the second man. This time, he fired before he could think about it. The first man doubled over and staggered back before falling, limp. Marcus turned back and drove the pistol hard against the pirate's temple. His victim slumped unconscious.

Marcus sagged against the console for a moment, working on catching his breath. He inspected his victims. Both were alive but unconscious, and the gunshot wound was bleeding like a son of a bitch. Guilt ripped at him. He'd just wanted to get to the radio. Killing someone was more than he wanted to accept responsibility for.

The radio. He crossed the room, flipped the controls as Brylie had instructed, then made the distress call.

"We received a distress call a few hours ago," the dispatcher told him. "The Southern Ocean Patrol is in route."

Relief shuddered through him. This would be over soon. But relief soon gave way to panic. He'd disabled the men who were piloting the Ice Queen. He may not have liked where they were going, but now— "There's no one available to steer this ship," he told the woman. "What the hell am I supposed to do?"

"Let me check the GPS you gave me."

He glanced toward the door. "Lady, I don't have all day. Someone's bound to come in." No point mentioning the gunfire. "I don't want to get caught here."

"Okay, you might be shallow enough that you can lower the anchor. Do you see the control for that?"

He scanned the controls—shit, there were a lot of them. "Yeah, I see it."

"It's just the press of a button."

The terrorists would notice when the ship stopped, but, hell, they would notice when their guys showed up with bullet holes, too. Marcus took a deep breath and pressed the button, heard the grinding beneath that was the chain being lowered. He had to get out of here now.

Scanning the room, he found two satellite phones. He tucked one in his pocket and balanced the other in his hand.

Shit, the gunshot victim was coming around and moaning. Marcus stared. He'd never shot a living thing before. He knelt beside the man and felt blood pooling, wet and sticky on his knees. Quickly, he assessed—where had the bullet struck? Chest? Gut? Leg?

Leg. How had that happened? His brother better never hear about that, since they'd gone to the shooting range for years. But yeah, he could help that wound. He pulled his belt free and looped it beneath the man's leg, close to his groin. He glanced at the other man, who was still out. He couldn't afford to spend any longer here. Someone no doubt heard the shots, or the chain, and would be on him in a matter of minutes. Once he tightened the belt, the blood flow slowed. He tied the leather, unwilling to waste more time, and wiped his hands on his jeans. That was the best he could do. He picked up the sat phone he'd set down beside him, then shoved the pirate's handgun along with the captain's in the back of his jeans. After a quick scan of the room, he collected the automatic weapon that had fallen under the console during the scuffle. One less weapon for the bad guys.

He needed to get back to Brylie in their new hiding place. He opened the door from the bridge, peered out, then bolted down the hall toward dry goods storage.

CHAPTER FOUR

Brylie had just entered dry goods storage where they'd decided to meet when she heard footsteps in the hall. Not taking time to see who it was, she vaulted toward one of the metal shelves, one weighted heavily on the bottom with bottled water. She grasped the post and hauled herself up. Her foot slipped on the shelf and her finger snagged on a piece of metal sticking out of the support. She stifled a cry of pain, holding her finger out as she hauled herself up. She hid behind tall boxes of toilet paper, wrapped her injured finger in the hem of her sweatshirt, and peered between the boxes.

Marcus staggered in, eyes wild, covered with blood.

This time she didn't muffle her cry, and she half jumped, half slid down the shelving, needing to touch him, to find out where he was hurt. Would she know enough to help him?

She hit the floor, the jolt running up her legs. Heart pounding, she stumbled forward and grasped his sweatshirt, her hands sliding beneath, looking for the wound. Her fingers encountered one of the pistols at the small of his back, and she snatched her hand away, then leaned back to inspect him. He looked so weary, the corners of his eyes drawn down, his brow lined, lips thin.

"Not my blood. I'm not hurt." He closed his hands around her arms, then released her immediately, but not before marking her sweatshirt with bloody handprints. "We need to get out of the line of sight." He urged her toward the shelves she'd just climbed down, but when she straightened, his gaze snapped to her own bloody shirt. "What happened?" He grabbed the front of her shirt, pulling it out to inspect it. He lifted his eyebrow in silent question.

"My finger. It's—it'll be fine." It burned like fire and a flap of skin hung loose. She had found a hiding place by the toilet paper—she could use that to wrap it until they could find something better. "You're not hurt."

"No. Come on. Can you climb?" He started up, held a hand to her.

She nodded. "I'm fine. Go."

God, so much blood on his clothes, on his jeans, his sweatshirt. Her heart hadn't slowed from her first glimpse of him coming through the door. She felt lightheaded and realized she'd been holding her breath, waiting for him to tell her what had happened.

Instead he took two pistols out of his belt and set them on top of one case while she opened another and pulled out a roll. He took the roll from her and pulled her finger into his lap.

"I heard shots," she said, not able to look at her finger now, not when he was willing to take care of it. "What happened?"

"Two guys were on the bridge, armed."

"And you shot them?"

The corner of his mouth turned up. "They shot first. I got their guns away. Hid one. Automatic weapon. Didn't think we could use it." He lifted his gaze to hers. "You need stitches, Bry."

She squeezed her eyes closed. "I know. I've had cuts before."

"I can find something to do the job in a bit. Kinda need to catch my breath."

She blew out a laugh, relieved when the breath left her lungs, and was replaced by cold air. "I bet."

He leaned against the wall beside the cardboard box of toilet paper. "The guys on the bridge—they can identify me. We need to keep a low profile for a bit."

"You made the call?"

"Made it and got these." He pulled out the two satellite phones and handed them over. "They're charged. I called the distress code you told me, and she told me someone had sent in a mayday call earlier, and S.O.P. is on the way. Now I want to call my brother and let him know what's going on. We should be okay soon."

"Oh!" She dove for his belt. He lifted his arms to accommodate her, his brow furrowed.

"What the hell?"

"The walkie. I need it." She snatched the radio out of his pocket.

"Where's yours?" He scanned the nest she'd made. "Did it die?"

"I rigged it so I could hear into the lounge."

"You did what?" He sat up, staring.

"I taped the button down and left it in the vent so we'll know what's going on."

His forehead smoothed and his lips quirked in admiration. "Good idea. But hell, Brylie, what if I'd tried to get in contact with you?"

"I had it with me until a few minutes ago. It should keep us in the loop until the battery runs out. But I needed to do something." She turned up the volume of his radio to listen in.

A jumble of sound reverberated in the open room and she adjusted the volume again. As she concentrated, she heard sobbing, and complaining, and finally the strident voices of the captors, the slamming of doors. They were no doubt looking for Marcus, though they didn't mention him by name, not yet, anyway. She shivered and Marcus rested his hand on her hip, drawing her against him. She moved into his warmth, the security of him, before he pulled his blood-stained hand away.

"Need to get cleaned up," he muttered, but his attention was on the walkie.

"Nowhere," an accented voice said.

"Get me the manifest," ordered another. "I want to see who is missing."

Brylie's knuckles tightened on the radio, and Marcus nudged her finger aside before she accidentally pressed the button. She could hardly catch her breath, she was so frightened. Would the others be punished for not revealing their absence?

Marcus rubbed his hand down her back as if that would calm her. Oddly, the simple contact did.

But just that made her feel guilty, for feeling secure while the others were in danger. She shifted to look at him, needing the whole story. "What exactly happened on the bridge?"

He shook his head, and for a moment, she thought he'd shut down. So the sound of his voice startled her, even though he pitched it low so they could hear the walkie.

"I never shot a man before. Christ, I didn't know what to do." He lifted a bloodstained hand to his face, stopping just before he touched it. "I just did what I'd seen in the movies, you know, to slow the bleeding. I didn't even stick around to see if it worked. And if the bullet's still in his leg, well, he's dead anyway, right?"

The pain in his eyes when he lifted his gaze to hers stabbed her in the heart. Despite the blood that flaked from his fingers, dried on his clothes, she nestled against him, folding her arms around him, pulling his head down to hers, her fingers moving over his hair.

"You did what you had to do," she murmured.

His breath blew against her throat, warm and damp, and then he pulled her closer, against the length of his body. For a moment she thought he wanted to lose himself in sex, but he just held her, smoothing his hand up and down her back, until the beating of his heart eased.

Shouting over the walkie made them both jolt and turn toward the radio. Rapid-fire Spanish poured out of the speaker and Marcus picked up the walkie, as if that would help him understand.

"*Sangre.* Blood," Brylie said. "*Pistola.* Not dead, though. I didn't hear the word for dead. They did say something about the anchor, though. They've raised it, presumably put their own man at the controls."

"Throw him overboard," the other voice said.

Brylie recoiled at the words. Was the man Marcus shot dead after all? She glanced at Marcus, who paled.

"Adolfo, please. We can call a helicopter to come get him," another, more reasonable voice said.

"And give away our location? No. Throw him overboard. And find the man who did this."

Goosebumps lifted all over Brylie's skin and she eased back into Marcus, who was shaking himself. When she looked up at him, she saw fury etched in the lines of his face, burning from his eyes.

"He's still alive," he said through lips that appeared frozen. "They're going to kill him."

"They. Not you."

"My fault, though."

"He would have shot you. You said so yourself."

"Or captured me and you would have been left alone."

She felt the tension ease from him, a little more with each passing moment. "You did the only thing you could."

"Doesn't really make me feel better." He bit off whatever else he was going to say when the shouting resumed.

The loud man, the apparent leader, said, "Bring me this man within the hour, or you're going into the water with Benito."

Brylie tensed and Marcus's arm tightened around her.

"They won't find us, we're well-hidden," he assured her. "Even if they get into the vents, they won't follow them here. We're safe for now."

She wished she could believe him, but the sounds coming over the radio contradicted him. She heard grumbles, shouts, and a crack. A moment passed before she realized someone had been slapped.

"You said she didn't get on in Hobart!" the leader, Adolfo, she knew now, shouted, his accent heavy.

The grumble of her father's voice responded. "She did not."

So that's how he was protecting her, as Monica had done this morning.

"Yet we have video of her last night on the deck with this man. Who is he?"

"It's too early in the cruise for me to know all the passengers."

Another crack. Was this man slapping her father? She could imagine her father's stoic reaction, his steely eyes.

"Who. Is. This. Man? He killed one of my men. Who is he? Who?"

"His name is Marcus Devlin." It was a man's voice, high pitched in panic. "You know, the Olympic snowboarder?"

"Devlin? The same Devlins that own this cruise line?"

"Oh, hell," Marcus muttered beside her. "My friend from the captain's table the other night. Fucker."

"Answer me!" Adolfo's voice grew louder, out of control.

"I'd heard we might get a visit from one of the members of the corporation," her father said, his tone resigned. "I didn't know it would be one of the family. He didn't introduce himself to me."

"Contact Devlin," Adolfo demanded. "Let him know his little brother picked a bad day for a cruise."

"No kidding," Marcus agreed.

"Let him know the demand has increased, now that I know a precious family member is on board. I want twenty million dollars for the safe return of the brat, the passengers and the ship."

"You should call your brother now," Brylie urged, shoving a phone toward him. "Find out what's going on with the rescue. They should be here soon, right? We just have to hide until they get here."

He picked up the phone and did as she asked while she held the radio to her ear, listening, but not hearing anything discernible. The leader's loud voice terrified her, but at least she knew what was going on.

Marcus did his best to hide his frustration from Brylie as he pressed Jessica, Harris's secretary, to put him through. Bad enough he had to suffer the delay on the phone as it relayed through the satellite, but he had to butt against Jessica, who didn't like him on the best of days, which this wasn't.

Okay, he probably deserved some of the attitude she threw at him, and he never did actually call when he didn't have a life-or-death sort of problem, only this time it was really life-or-death and she was blocking him.

"He's got other problems to deal with right now, Marcus," Jessica was saying.

He pictured her sitting in her office, blonde hair coiled atop her head, blouse buttoned to her chin, at odds with the short skirts she usually wore. Great legs, too. She might like him better if he'd followed through on his flirting and actually gave her a tumble, but he got the feeling Harris was already going there, something his wife Teresa would not like.

"I know all about the cruise ship problem because I'm on it," he told her.

"You are not. How can you be calling?"

"Long story, Jess, look, just put me through, will you? I need to know what's going on with the rescue efforts. Are they on their way?"

"He's on the other line just now, Marcus. I'll put you through as soon as he's done." She ended the call without another word, and he blinked at the phone. Right. On hold. Weird to be hearing instrumental '80s music over the phone when he was being hunted by bad guys.

Finally, Harris came on. "Marcus! You're safe?"

"For now."

"I was just on the phone with Adolfo. He made me think he had you right there."

"On a first name basis with terrorists, bro?"

Marcus could see Harris scowl from here. "Of course not. It's how he introduced himself to me. So you're not there with him?"

"I'm hidden for the time being, me and the chef. He has other people with him, though, all the passengers and crew. I think he has one of his men operating the ship. Did you get in touch with the authorities? I called them from the radio on the bridge. I don't know how much longer we can hide."

"Southern Ocean Maritime Patrol and Response are on their way."

Marcus swore. "Aren't they the ones who report poaching or whatever? This is a bit bigger than that."

"I know, but they're the closest, as I said. And they're armed. Do you know how many pirates are on board?"

Marcus shook his head, though he realized his brother couldn't see. "No. We can't see into the lounge, and we've been trying to keep a low profile. So no telling where they are. I do have the call sign of their ship. Got a pen?" He rattled off the number and letters, and met Brylie's surprised gaze.

"They're not going to stop looking until they find you, now that they know who you are," Harris said.

"I know. So make sure help gets here soon, all right? And remind me to kick your ass for putting me on this ship to begin with."

He hung up but didn't look at Brylie. He lifted his hand to pass through his head and stopped when he caught sight of the blood of the man he'd shot. It had dried on his skin and shirt, making it stiff, and Christ, it smelled. He shoved himself toward the edge of the shelf, needing to get away from her, not wanting her to smell the violence on him, not wanting it to touch her.

"I need to wash this off me." He grasped the post of the shelving unit and swung himself to the ground, remembering only at the last minute he needed to keep quiet.

After scouring the shelves, he found some bottled water and carried it to stand over a drain in the floor. Using his teeth to uncap it, he poured it over his hands, rubbing them together, and watched the red liquid spiral and disappear down the drain.

Brylie appeared at his side and he spun on her, defensive, and mad at himself. He hadn't even heard her climb down.

He scowled. "You're going to get caught. Get back up there where it's safe."

She said nothing, didn't even acknowledge that she heard him, just handed him some wadded toilet tissue. She took the bottle of water from him and poured as he scrubbed the endless blood from the creases of his hand. He resisted the urge to grab another bottle when the first was empty, but they needed to conserve, just in case. He scrubbed his hands until the toilet tissue fell apart, then he stepped back.

Brylie crouched to mop up the clumps of tissue and the wetness around the drain with more toilet tissue. She straightened and tucked the pinkened paper away before leaving him standing there at the drain, wondering what the hell he'd done right in his life to be stranded here with her.

***

Marcus woke from a dream where he was falling, sliding off his bed. He opened his eyes in the darkened room and realized it wasn't a dream. The ship was listing, and he and Brylie were sliding off their perch on the top shelf.

He wrapped one arm around her and reached out with his other hand, spreading his legs at the same time, hoping some part of his body would catch some part of the shelving before they slid the fifteen feet to the floor below. Just when he felt his feet dangle over the edge without catching anything, the ship rolled in the other direction, sending them tumbling into the wall. Brylie twisted and flung her hands out. He felt the jolt in her body as a case of God-knew-what slammed against her.

"Okay?" he muttered. "What is it?"

"I think we've hit the Drake Passage. The seas get rough here. We need to get down." She broke away and moved toward the edge of the shelf. "The shelves should stay, and most of this stuff is secured but—."

He got it. Too many projectiles. He snatched up the walkie and the guns, tucked them in his clothing, and followed her down the shelves, feeling his way in the dark. Another pitch of the ship and his feet slipped out from under him and he gripped the upright pole with both hands.

"Brylie!"

"I'm okay. I'm down."

He felt her hands on his legs, guiding him to the next shelf. He balanced himself with a quick touch of the sole of his foot to the shelf and jumped the rest of the way to the floor as the ship rolled. He stumbled and she caught him. The supplies shifting on the shelves made him nervous.

"Let's go." He closed his hand around her arm and guided her toward the door.

She dug her feet in. "Where?"

"Someplace where shit won't fall on our heads. Someone's bunk should be nearby, right?"

"Yes, but—"

"Surely they won't come looking for us in this." Behind him something crashed to the ground and skidded across the floor. His shoulders tightened as he waited for the next projectile to land on him. "Come on. Let's go."

They pushed through the door of dry storage and into the hall. Even the dim hall lights hurt his eyes after straining to see in the darkness of the hold.

She turned to the first door on the right and used her master key card. He braced his legs apart and pressed his hand against her back to steady her. She pushed the door open and they staggered in. He turned quickly, shut the door quietly and applied the safety lock. When he turned back, he saw Brylie bent over the full-sized bunk, pulling straps from the wall beside the mattress.

"Did we walk into the fetish room here?" he teased.

"Keeps you from rolling out of bed during rough seas," she retorted. "Feels like this may be more than just the passage. I think we've run into a storm." Once the straps were in place she leaned over the bed to look out the rain-and-wave-lashed windows. "I wish we could see the radar, to see how big it is."

"Yeah, I'm not going back on the bridge." He sat on the edge of the bed and removed his boots with a sigh. "We can just pretend we're living a hundred years ago and ride the storm out."

"What are you doing?" she asked when he stood and unbuttoned his jeans.

He shoved the stiff fabric down his legs. "Going to take a shower. Can't bear having this blood on me anymore."

"It's not really safe to shower in the middle of this."

"You don't have a strap in there to hold me to the wall?" He grinned and stood to strip off his sweatshirt. "See if whoever room this is has some pants I can wear."

"Oh, please let them be pink." She stumbled two steps to the closet.

He opened a drawer and dropped the walkie, the sat phones and the gun inside before closing it again, securing it. "You'll be okay?"

She glanced toward the door and swallowed. "Sure."

He got the feeling she wanted to say something else but though he waited, she didn't add anything, just gave him a nervous smile, so he slipped into the bathroom.

God, it felt good to get the crusty blood off his skin, though he had to resist the urge to scrub until his skin was raw. He felt it everywhere, could see it every time he closed his eyes. But after being jostled around the shower like a ball in one of those kids' toys that toddlers pushed around—one of the pitches of the ship sent him slamming into the nozzles, ow—he shut off the water, toweled off and opened the door to see Brylie sitting on the bed, clutching the window ledge as she watched the tossing sea. He studied her for a moment, her expression peaceful, which surprised the hell out of him, considering the way the boat tossed.

She turned to him with a smile, different than the one she'd sent him into the shower with. This was more the Brylie he'd known before all this shit went down.

"I found you some sweats, pants and a shirt." She nodded toward the chair at the end of the bed, then turned her attention back to the sea. "They might be too big."

"No problem." He dropped his towel, with no reaction from her. He reached for his shorts, then the gray sweats. "Must be some storm."

"It's pretty incredible." She looked over her shoulder and her eyes widened.

He stopped with his shorts halfway up. "Should I stop?"

She flicked her gaze to the door. "No. I wouldn't be able to relax."

"Oh, yeah you would." But he got it. Not the right time. He pulled the pants up the rest of the way. They were a little loose and long. He searched for the string to pull the waistband tight. "Once this is over, I'm taking you back to that hotel and keeping you there for a week."

"What?" She tucked her hair behind her ear as she turned to face him. "What?"

He sat beside her and drew that same lock of hair free to rub it between his fingers. He loved her hair, soft and floaty. "I want to keep you in a room, to myself, no one looking for us, for a week. Maybe two."

She laughed and drew away, sitting with her head against the wall, that same Mona Lisa smile playing on her lips as she looked at him. "You would get bored."

"I don't think so." He grabbed his sweatshirt and drew it over his chilled skin. Then he edged further onto the bed and wrapped his arms around her so they could watch the tossing sea together.

"The passengers are going to get seasick," she murmured. "I hope the gunmen let Joan distribute the medicine."

He passed a soothing hand down her hip. "I'm sure they will, or they'll be the ones dealing with the puking."

"Maybe we should listen to know what's going on." She twisted to reach for the drawer.

He tightened his arms around her. "Nothing you can do about it anyway. Why torture yourself?"

"It's wrong that I'm safe and they're not."

"They are. They'll be safe as long as these men want their money. They might not be comfortable or happy, but they're safe." He smoothed her hair against her temple and she dropped her head against his shoulder. "When the storm passes, the patrol will be here and this will be over." He didn't voice his own fear that the storm would delay their rescue further. She'd figure that out for herself soon enough.

The ship pitched and rolled violently. Marcus felt like a giant hand was picking them up and dropping them down, sometimes so far on the side he thought they might capsize. He tightened his grip on Brylie, as if he could protect her if that happened.

"Are you okay?" he asked, as his stomach did a tumble rivaling the time he did a 1080 rotation on the half-pipe.

"Ugh, that was a bad one." She reached behind her for the strap and pulled it across them. "Buckle us in."

"I liked it better when I thought these had another purpose." He found the connection and made it so the strap pinned their hips to the bunk. She handed him the next strap and he buckled it over their chests. "Shit. I feel like a bug on a board at a science fair."

"Now you can fall asleep without worrying about falling out of bed. You can face this way."

He turned, but couldn't keep his gaze on her, not when she tilted at crazy angles. "Oh, geez," he groaned, and shifted onto his back to stare at the ceiling. "Have you been in a storm like this before?"

"There's always a chop when we pass the 50th parallel, but no. Not like this."

He turned his head to look at her. "So you have a gut of iron, then."

"I'm trying to impress you." She couldn't hide her smile.

The ship nosed into a trough, practically standing them on their heads and he bit out a groan. "I'm impressed." Much more of that and he'd disgrace himself. "How long do these things usually last?"

"Hours. Sometimes a lot of hours."

He rested his forearm over his eyes. "That was just mean."

"Do you want me to lie?" She shifted onto her side and placed her hand on his chest.

He covered her hand with his, rubbed his fingertips over the soft skin, tapping her knuckles. "Maybe."

"So I should have said it'll be over in ten minutes and then everyone gets a cookie?"

"Crème brulee," he corrected with a grin.

"All right then. You don't puke on me and I'll get you some crème brulee."

"Maybe that Antarctica beer would be a better idea," he muttered when the bed angled. "You think they'd let your dad out to pilot us through this? He's been through shit like this before, yeah?"

"He's been doing this for years, and was in the Navy before that. So, yeah." She smoothed her hand over his chest, as if that would soothe him. "I would have thought a man with your adventurous spirit would like this. It's kind of like a ride."

He chuckled. "Never done something quite this insane." He wouldn't think about the ship turning over into the icy seas. He never should have watched that Titanic movie, even for the special effects. All he could see was Leonardo clinging to that damned chunk of ice. "Are there icebergs out there?"

"Not usually this far north. Relax. Try to get some rest."

Funny how she was telling him to relax now, but he liked the sound of her voice, imagined it was pitched low for another reason than to avoid detection by any bad guys that might be lurking in the hall. "It'd be like sleeping on a damned roller coaster."

***

"Tell me some of the crazy things you've done. They have to be worse than this."

He let his fingers travel up her arm as he returned his gaze to the ceiling, needing a focal point that wasn't moving. He understood what she was doing, and appreciated it. His mind needed something besides the storm and the pirates to focus on. And maybe if he remembered his wilder stunts, this might not seem so bad. Only he'd been the one calling the shots then. "Let's see. I've surfed in Teahupoo, Tahiti, which has some of the most extreme waves in the world. I jumped out of a helicopter to ski down a mountain in New Zealand."

"Oh, my God."

He chuckled, feeling the air sucked out of his lungs even three years after the stunt. "Yeah, that was something I won't do again. Oh, and I was in the delivery room with my sister when she had her first baby. That was pretty terrifying, especially when she damn near ripped my arm off."

"And you're scared of a little thunder and lightning?" She shifted closer and turned her gaze to him. "How did you happen to be in the delivery room with your sister?"

"Her husband was out of town. The kid was early by about three weeks. Mom and Dad were on a cruise, Jimmy was in San Francisco. I was all she had."

"Surely not. She wanted you in there. Women don't just invite people willy-nilly into the delivery room."

"Maybe she wanted to scare me straight so I wouldn't knock anybody up." He dug tickling fingers into the soft flesh of her side.

She laughed and jerked away. "Maybe you made her feel safe."

He snorted, but another roll of the ship had him reaching for the buckles. He dragged himself free from the straps and made it to the bathroom just in time.

No crème brulee for him.

A rustling by the door told him Brylie had joined him. He waved a hand behind him, not wanting to remove his head from the vicinity of the toilet. "Go away, Brylie. You're going to get hurt."

Why he thought she'd start listening to him now, he had no idea. She braced her hand on the wall beside him and ran the water in the tiny sink to his left. Before he could open his mouth to protest, she pressed a cool cloth to his head. Who knew such a gesture could feel like heaven? He pressed his hand over hers to hold it in place, and closed his eyes. A toss of the ship sent her lurching to the side. Moments later, she closed the door, then he felt her settle behind him, her legs folded around his hips, her cheek against his back, also amazingly soothing. Her fingers stroked the back of his neck until he felt his stomach settle.

"I feel like an idiot."

"I won't tease you until tomorrow," she promised.

He groaned, and with extreme humiliation, puked again.

When Brylie woke the next morning, Marcus was no longer clammy under her hand, and his breathing was even, relaxed. She wished this was a normal morning, that they could wake slowly, leisurely. But if this was a normal morning, they wouldn't be here, would they? She stroked her finger down his back, then turned carefully so she wouldn't disturb him.

The seas were decidedly calmer, though a glance out the window told her they were still plenty rough, and the clouds still appeared turbulent.

"Their ship is gone," she said aloud as soon as she realized it.

"What?" Marcus twisted on the bunk to look at her, then the window. He sat up and leaned across her for a closer look, then scrambled off the bed, groaning at the movement.

"Where are you going?" she demanded when he shoved his feet in his shoes.

He turned with his finger to his lips. Right. Now that the storm had died down, they needed to be quiet. And hidden. Her stomach fluttered with fear and she wished they were safe in their hiding place.

"I'm going to see." He tightened his laces with a yank.

"Wait." She stretched toward the drawer and opened it with a pop, the contents sliding around. She winced at the sound. She drew out the walkie and carefully turned up the volume. Her heart squeezed when she heard nothing.

"Maybe the other walkie is dead. Or they're still asleep."

Or gone. On the other ship.

"We have to know." She crawled off the bed and sought her own shoes.

"Uh-uh. I'm putting you back above the freezer. It's the safest place."

She stilled and stared. "You're not going to pull that macho crap now, are you?"

He straightened and returned her gaze. "We have no idea what we're going to find. They could be asleep, or they could be gone." He stopped himself, swallowing.

"They could be dead."

Shaking his head, he turned to his other boot. "I don't think they are. Why would they be? No benefit to the pirates then. I just—I may need to do things and I don't want you implicated." As if to make it clear, he pulled one of the guns from the drawer. He held it in front of him, checked the safety with more assurance than she was comfortable with. He turned back to her. "Please."

She had to hide her fear that he wouldn't return, that he would be captured and she wouldn't be able to help him, that she wouldn't know what to do to help him. "Leave me the other gun."

"Hell no." He stood, tried to tuck the gun in the back of his sweatpants, but they were too loose. He swore, shucked them and grabbed his bloody jeans, the fabric stiff and crusty. He buttoned them and secured the pistol in the waistband.

"I know how to use it. My father was in the Navy, remember, and when I moved to New York, he insisted I be licensed to have one in my apartment."

"Not the same."

"Oh, really? Using it to defend myself?"

His jaw tightened and he kept his gaze averted. "You don't know what it's like to shoot someone. I don't want you to know. So I'm keeping the gun."

"Would you rather I know what it's like to be dead? Or worse?"

His gaze snapped to hers, the lines on his face tight, as if he hadn't considered that. Lips thinned, he took one pistol and handed it to her, grip first. Her own shoulders tense, she released the magazine to check, tapped it back into place, then pulled back the slide, keeping the barrel pointed down. When she looked up again, she saw approval in his eyes, and he'd relaxed just a bit.

"You ready?" He held a hand out to her.

She thought, just for a moment, that she'd tuck her hands on the mattress under her and refuse to move. They were safe here for the moment. They were together. Instead, she tucked away the pistol, picked up the walkie in one hand, put her other in his and followed him into the hall and back into the vent.

***

Marcus would feel better once she was safely back on the freezer, then…Christ, he didn't know what he'd do. He had to do something, and he had to do it without worrying about Brylie.

Though he would anyway. But if the hostages were dead, he didn't want her to see that. If he had to act, he didn't want her to see that, either. Bad enough he had to live with it.

"Right. I'll be back as soon as I can. Use the satellite phone and call the Southern Ocean Patrol, see what their status is."

Without waiting for acknowledgement, without a kiss that would keep her in his head, he headed back through the vent toward the lounge.

He heard the accented voices before he reached the lounge, and relief poured through him. Not that he wanted to encounter these bastards, but thinking about being on the ship, just him and Brylie in the middle of the ocean, had creeped the hell out of him. So, still in danger, but not alone. He edged nearer and looked through the vent the best he could. All the passengers sat on the floor by the inner wall, from what he could see, and the furniture was gone. Out of the way, maybe, because of the storm. He could see that older couple from the States, the woman with her head on her husband's shoulder, her eyes shadowed as he curved his hand around her head protectively. One of the three adventurers sat nearby, his jaw set mutinously. Where were his companions? Marcus knew that look. He'd seen it in the mirror often enough. It was the look of a guy about to do something stupid.

Please don't let him do anything stupid.

He wished he could see Brylie's dad, but the captain was probably on the bridge. Had the man had any sleep? Marcus felt a twinge of guilt for his own restful night, with Brylie's arms around him.

He didn't see Trinity, or the asshole from dinner. A thought occurred to him and he reached for the radio Brylie had left here. Shit, where was it? Of course, they hadn't secured it. It probably slid all over the place during the storm. No telling where it was now. Great. Their one connection to the pirates and it was lost.

At least he knew what the silence meant now.

Ah, well, the battery was bound to run out sooner or later. Now that he knew everyone was safe, for the most part, he needed to get back to Brylie. Hopefully she'd reached the Southern Ocean Patrol and would have good news, like rescue was on the bloody horizon.

Before he went back, though, he wanted to know where the pirates' ship was. He hadn't seen it through the porthole. They may have just untethered it for the duration of the storm, but he wanted to be sure. That meant going out on deck and exposing himself to danger.

And since he had no way to contact Brylie, she was going to kick his ass for making her worry.

Nonetheless, he made his way through the vent to one of the doors that exited the ship opposite the side the pirates had boarded. His muscles strained as he lowered himself through the panel after checking for intruders. If he was lucky, they'd be as messed up as he was after last night. In fact, now might be the right time for a diversion that could have the pirates on the run once and for all. If only he had a way to get in contact with the people inside the lounge. He'd bet those adventure boys would go for it, and maybe even the asshole.

The captain, maybe. He'd check the bridge after this, see how guarded Brylie's dad was.

Yeah, Brylie was going to kick his ass if he didn't get back to her soon, but he could sure move a hell of a lot faster without worrying about her keeping up.

He opened the same door he'd exited before, since it hadn't alerted the pirates last time. He sucked in a sharp breath as the dry air struck him. Christ it was cold, and the thick sweatshirt he wore offered no protection against the wind. He tucked his hands into his sleeves and kept close to the outside of the ship, aware of windows that would give him away.

The ocean still churned, keeping him off balance, all of it gray, so he could hardly tell where the sky began. He couldn't watch it long or he'd be on his knees puking again. Still, it was gorgeous in its violence, in its wildness. He almost wished Brylie was here to see it.

But no, this was too dangerous. No ship in sight this way. He considered rounding the front of the ship, but feared being detected. He'd go to the rear, though it was a greater distance. He'd be exposed longer. His gut tightening, he drew the gun and edged along the ship, every muscle ready for action, every nerve straining for a sign of the bad guys.

He caught sight of the stern of the other ship before he reached the end of the icebreaker. The pirates' vessel was a couple dozen meters out. This time he saw movement, men walking about on deck securing the ship. He counted seven.

He considered the pistol in his hand, but decided against using it. He was no crack shot, and even if he was, the distance was too great. He needed to get back to Brylie. Also, he was starving after emptying his stomach last night. He was glad she'd thought to hide food. He just needed to make his way back to it.

First he wanted to check on the bridge, see if he could get a better headcount of the hostage takers there, because no doubt the captain was operating the ship and was surely being guarded. Gun at the ready, he reentered the hallway, deciding not to go back in the vent just yet. His muscles were still a bit watery from his illness and he couldn't climb as easily. So he'd creep and take his chances.

A couple of wrong turns later—he'd maneuvered through the vents more than the hallways in his short time on board—he reached the hallway leading to the bridge. He swore. He wasn't going to be able to approach without leaving himself vulnerable. If the door to the bridge opened, he'd have no time to get into the storage room and he'd be screwed. But he needed to act.

Gun balanced in his hand, he approached the door, nerves snapping through him, worse than that time he'd jumped out of the helicopter on his snowboard. Every sound triggered the flight urge in his legs, his entire body poised to take off the opposite direction.

Then he reached the door and lifted himself to look in the narrow horizontal window. He saw three men in the room from that vantage point, none of them the captain. What did that mean? Of course, he didn't know just where the captain would be situated. And he could only see the backs of the other men's heads, no telling if they were friend or foe.

He'd count them as foe, because if the good guys had taken over, wouldn't Brylie's dad have come looking for her?

Right. Nothing he could do here now. Time to go back and pass the information he had on to the authorities.

He hurried back down the hall and turned the corner just as he heard the snick of a door opening.

CHAPTER FIVE

Shit. Shit. The sound of footsteps followed the closing of the door—not someone who was trying to be quiet. So, a pirate. No way was Marcus going to be able to get in the vents with someone coming down the hall. He tugged the master key card Brylie had given him out of his pocket and scanned the hallway for what he thought might be the safest door. Pivoting, knowing he was running out of time before the footsteps rounded the corner, he slid the keycard in the slot of the first door he came across.

A red light flashed.

Fuck.

He hurried down to the next door, tried it again with hands shaking. Red light again. Had the pirates figured they were hiding in the rooms and deactivated the card? He wasn't going to chance it. He'd just haul ass, leading them away from the kitchen and Brylie.

Come on, asshole.

"Hey!"

The shouted warning galvanized him. He sprinted forward, around the corner, then the next, wondering how the hell he was going to buy time with a malfunctioning key card.

He heard the footsteps speed up behind him, but didn't hear others join it. Right. He could deal with one guy. He pulled to a halt around the corner and waited, listening to the footsteps approach. Taking a deep breath, he pivoted into the path of his pursuer. He had only a split second to adjust his stance, correct his aim before he slammed his fist into the man's face.

He felt the crunch of cartilage—he knew the feeling well enough—and the snap of something else, followed by a sharp pain in the back of his hand. *Fuck*. Had he broken his goddamned hand?

But he'd laid out the bad guy on the ground. He knew the guy wouldn't stay there, so he raised the gun and slammed the butt against the guy's temple. Tucking the gun in the back of his pants, he straddled the limp body. With quick movements he patted the guy down, netting a radio, sat phone and two more guns.

He didn't have enough pockets and damn, his hand hurt. So he'd keep the phone and radio and ditch the guns, first chance he got. But now he had to beat it before this guy's friends came to look for him.

***

Brylie sat forward when she heard the noise in the vent. She let out her breath on a rush when Marcus's face appeared. He was pale, but when he reached her, he curved one hand around the back of her head and covered her mouth with his. His kiss was hard and hot and deep, his tongue pushing into her mouth as if he was starving for her. Not knowing why, she nonetheless angled her head and leaned back, wanting the reassurance of his weight over her. He was back, he was safe, and something had him ramped up. Her hands skimmed over him, searching for injury, dreading finding one.

But he didn't flinch when she touched him, instead followed her down. He made a strangled sound before he flipped onto his back, staring at the ceiling.

"What's wrong?" She leaned over him, studying his drawn face in the dim light. She must have missed an injury somewhere.

He drew his hand up to rest on his chest. "Messed up my hand."

"What?" She straightened. "How?"

"Punched a guy." He sat up, putting some distance between them, and pulled the radio and sat phone from his jeans and placed them beside him.

"What? Who?"

He told her what had happened.

"Your key card isn't working anymore."

Her stomach dropped. "My—it's not? Are you sure?"

"Yeah, when I was trying to hide earlier, I was going to slip into one of the rooms, but the lock stayed red. I tried it on more than one room, too," he said when she opened her mouth to suggest just that. "My thought was that they deactivated all the key cards when they realized we were missing."

"So we're stuck here."

"Only until help arrives." He stroked her hair back from her face. "I took a couple of their automatic weapons and ditched them in a linen closet, too. I couldn't carry them, but didn't want them to have them. Was worried you'd be pissed at me for taking so long."

She caught his hand in both of hers, pulled it into her lap and looked into his eyes. "You had me in knots worrying. And apparently with good reason. Did you see my dad?"

"No. I didn't see any of our crew, not in the lounge or on the bridge."

"Do you think they're still on the ship?"

"The hostages are. I don't know why they'd separate the crew. They're bound to still be here."

The warmth she'd felt from his kiss evaporated as her fear rose again. "They'd keep him. They need him."

"Right." His finger twirled around a lock of her hair. "Don't worry."

Easier said than done. Even easier when she had something else to worry about. "What about your hand?"

He grimaced as he held it up. "I don't think it's broken. Bruised pretty bad, though."

"I thought you'd know how to punch someone without hurting yourself."

He snorted. "Yeah, well, I kinda was moving on the fly. What did you find out from the S.O.P.?"

Her mouth tightened. "The storm blew them off course, and us. They're trying to find us but it's going to be awhile, maybe even tomorrow."

"We can hang on until tomorrow." He sat against the wall, wincing as he cradled his hand.

"Marcus. Are you sure it's not broken?"

"I've had a broken hand before. Feels different."

"Snowboarding or fighting?" She didn't know why it mattered, but she wanted to know.

He met her gaze. "What do you think?"

His admission of violence should bother her, but after the past few days, she couldn't let it. He was the person she was trusting to get her through this. She wasn't going to judge his past. "It could be a different bone."

"I don't think—"

His words were cut off by a screeching sound that Brylie finally realized was the intercom. Hope bloomed. Her father? Did they have control of the ship? An echoing silence filled the room before a booming voice spoke, the words bouncing off the close walls of the hiding space.

"Marcus Devlin, your presence is required in the lounge. Trust me when I say, you will be much happier if you come to us than if we have to come to you."

The intercom cut off.

Marcus focused on Brylie, watched her face grow pale and her eyes widen. He covered her hand with his. "He won't find us." His grip gentled on hers as he felt her pulse race. "Or it will take him some time. Don't worry."

God, he was such a liar. How could he tell her not to worry when he had no idea what this man wanted, other than him? When he knew the man threw his own man overboard. Yeah, he was worth more alive than dead, but he *had* taken out a few of the pirates, and alive was a relative term.

He folded his arms on his knees and dropped his forehead to them. Waiting wasn't his strong point, either.

"Without the other walkie, we won't know what's going on." She held up the lone radio.

"No." He rubbed the knuckle of his good thumb between his eyes. "Wait." He straightened and grabbed the radio he'd taken from the man in the hall. He inspected the controls and turned up the volume. "We can hear them communicating with each other."

Her expression still wary as she eyed the device, she relaxed her shoulders a little. "As long as they're talking to each other."

He gave her a crooked grin. "Patience."

She rolled her head and tried to return his smile. "I'm ready for this to be over."

He could end it now. He could turn himself in. but he'd have to leave her alone, and he wasn't prepared to do that. Besides, he got the feeling she wouldn't stay put, stay safe, and he couldn't protect her if he was a hostage.

They'd wait. But Christ, it felt like his nerves were on the outside of his skin.

He didn't realize he was cradling his hand until she said, "I have a first aid kit in the kitchen. There's some ibuprofen."

He shook his head. "I don't want you out of my sight. I'll be fine. I snowboarded with a broken collarbone, a broken arm, a broken rib."

She folded her legs and rested her head against the wall, settling in. "Is there anything you haven't broken?"

He chuckled. "Very little. My neck, though it's been a near thing. My left hip. My jaw."

Her eyes widened at the short list. "How many concussions have you had?"

"Three."

"With a helmet?"

He winked. "Sure." He pointed to his right eye socket. "Crushed this. Broke my nose a few times. Both shins, different times. Ah. I haven't broken my right femur. My right foot. My right knee dislocated."

"No wonder you retired."

"That's not why."

"So? Why?"

He shrugged and looked at her sideways. "Stopped being fun. Started being a job."

"God forbid."

He grinned. "I like to be entertained."

She swept her hand at their surroundings. "Entertaining enough for you?"

"You bet. Think I'm too old to be a—what's the ship equivalent of air marshal?"

A series of popping sounds jarred them. Marcus jerked into a sitting position, his entire body tight.

"What was it?"

He didn't want to say, didn't want to make it real. His blood was icy in his veins.

"Was it gunshots?"

"That's what it sounded like." He couldn't stay still any longer, and lunged for the vent, though navigating it would be a challenge with his hand. "Stay here."

"Oh, no. My father—"

"Damn it, Brylie." But she was right. He couldn't leave her alone, not and be able to think about the bad guys. "Jesus. Stay close. I'm serious." His heart thundered. He couldn't protect her, not against bullets. He wanted to lock her in the damn freezer, keep her there until he figured out what was going on, until he could—hell, he couldn't do anything. Frustration tensed his muscles. Why wasn't he trained for this? Maybe he should have just let the terrorists take them with the others. At least they knew rescue was on the way.

He headed through the now-familiar vent, careful not to put too much weight on his hand. The sound of shouts carried as they got closer to the lounge, most of it in Spanish. The pirates were yelling at each other. He wished to hell he spoke Spanish. He heard sobs, too, a woman— no, more than one woman. And a keening.

He almost didn't want to look through the vent. But he sucked in a deep breath and looked down into chaos.

Blood spattered the wall across from the vent—a lot of blood. No one was in sight, though he could hear the shouting below him, and the crying. He tried to remember how many shots he'd heard. Not enough to take out all the passengers, but how many?

He glanced back at Brylie, whose anxious face was lit in stripes through the vent. If only there was another way to see into the room. Jesus, that was a lot of blood. He forced himself to listen past the buzz in his ears to the chaos below.

"Jesus! He's dying! God! We have to stop the bleeding!" An American voice, a man, high in panic.

Some Spanish, or whatever. He caught the word *pistola*. Babbling of, "Oh, my God, oh, my God," over and over. Nothing that gave him any clue over who'd been shot, who had done the shooting, what had provoked it. He sensed Brylie moving away and glanced over his shoulder.

"I've got to see that my father is okay," she whispered.

He followed her down the vent, far enough that he felt safe talking, though he hated leaving without knowing what had happened. He grasped her wrist in the narrow passageway, jerking her to a stop.

"And how are you going to see without putting yourself at risk? Without putting us both at risk?"

"At risk?" She spoke through her teeth, her eyes flashing anger and contempt.

"He's my father."

"And he'd want you safe. Let me think. Let me think. There has to be a way to find out what's going on in there. Someone's hurt pretty bad."

"I know. I heard. Marcus, those are my friends down there."

"So what do you want to do, just run in there? You know this ship better than I do. Think." He tightened his grip on her wrist.

She looked ready to cry, and he regretted his harsh tone. He released her and sat against the side of the vent. "I've got to go back and hear what's going on. I need to know you're going to be safe. Don't go trying to find your dad, all right?"

She set her jaw, and for a moment he thought she was going to tell him to fuck himself. Instead she said, "I'm coming with you."

He nodded, not acknowledging the relief that poured through him. Good. He headed toward the lounge.

He eased to one side so that Brylie could squeeze up beside him and listen to what was going on below.

"You have to call a medevac helicopter," a man's voice below them pleaded. "We have to get him out of here or we're going to lose him. You can't afford to let him die."

Huh. That was a weird thing to say. Marcus knew the voice, too. He couldn't place it, but he'd heard it. He mentally revisited the people he'd spoken with on the ship in the short time he'd been on board, but couldn't match the face with the voice.

"We will not risk calling anyone. Already we've been compromised with the incident on the bridge. Our time is running out."

Marcus frowned. Not an accented voice. Was someone on board working with the pirates?

"The medevac chopper can bring the ransom and you can go."

"You think they'll just send the money along?" This time, an accented voice chimed in. "No. we stick with the original plan. Though I want Marcus Devlin here to ensure I get what I want. He's making too much trouble out there."

"He's an idiot, Hilario. Just some rich kid playing hide and seek."

Marcus tensed at the voice of the man who addressed the pirate. The douche from the captain's table the first night. He was working with the pirates? He knew the leader's first name. His questions made sense now, the questions about security and the threat, gauging their preparedness, but Marcus wouldn't have thought he'd have the balls to act.

"I say we get what we can from the passengers and go," another accented voice said. "We already lost Enrique and if this man dies, we're murderers."

What man? Marcus willed someone to give the man's identity, but instead he heard the sound of flesh to flesh, and a grunt. Someone had made their opinion of the reasonable man's opinion known.

"It's his own fault," the douche said. "He rushed you. What did he think would happen?"

One of the adventurers, Marcus reasoned. But was anyone else hurt? He didn't hear the crying woman anymore, or the sound of any other voices below him. And Douche was being pretty open about his association with the pirates. Marcus doubted he'd do that in front of the other passengers. So maybe they'd been moved, but where? It'd have to be the dining room. Just when he wanted to ask Brylie if they'd have a better view of the dining room, the men below him got quiet, and he couldn't risk speaking. He didn't want to move.

"Do you know who that is?" Brylie asked, close to his ear so it was more breath than words.

He nodded again. She eased back to look into his face questioningly, but he didn't dare speak. He could enlighten her later.

"I can go look for Devlin, bring him in," another voice said.

"No. I want you where I can keep an eye on you. He'll come in on his own. He'll have to."

Below them, he heard the men move away, and he shoved Brylie's hips in a signal to head back. They wouldn't learn anything else here.

***

"They shot one of those four kids," she said when they were huddled back on the freezer. She was shaking with a bone deep chill that had nothing to do with the temperature. They hadn't been able to reach the dining room through the vent. She had no idea how they'd know what was going on now.

"He was a man, not a kid, and he tried to take out a guy with a gun. Not the smartest thing."

"You went up against men with guns," she retorted. "That could have been you."

His jaw tightened, as if he hadn't considered that. Of course he wouldn't. He charged down snowy hills at sixty miles per hour. That the young man had acted on impulse was something Marcus should understand very well.

"The man they were talking to was the asshole from my table the first night, the one who kept asking about the pirate threat. There was another voice, too, but I couldn't place it. And I counted four shots. We don't know if anyone else was hurt."

"I want to go check on my dad. While everyone's distracted, now might be the time to go."

He blew out a frustrated breath, his mouth grim. "We need to know who else is helping them. You don't know that other voice?"

She shook her head.

"I think it's an employee, which means you'd know better than I."

She shook her head. "I didn't recognize it." What good would it do to know anyway? It wouldn't help them out of this mess.

"Marcus Devlin," a voice boomed over the intercom, making them jump. "One of your passengers is dead and another gravely wounded. It is up to you whether or not I dump them over the side of the ship. Meet me in the dining room in fifteen minutes, or the wounded man goes over."

Marcus swore, low and deep, and hi body tensed. She grabbed his arm as he shifted toward the opening of the vent. "Don't even think about it."

He turned to her, his eyes bright with pain. "And what? Let them throw another wounded man over the side? This one is my responsibility. He paid to go on my ship."

Terror squeezed her chest, made it difficult to speak. She couldn't let him go. She'd never see him again. She was certain of that. "So you're just going to march in there and hand yourself over to men with guns? What's stopping them from killing you?"

"My name." He pitched his voice to soothe. It didn't work. "They won't get the payout they want without me."

"They can still hurt you and get it."

"A chance I'll have to take." He gave her that damned tilted grin. "I've been hurt before. I can deal."

She tensed when he removed the pistol from the small of his back and placed it on top of the freezer.

"You know how to use this."

Okay, reason didn't work. She'd use guilt. "You are not leaving me out here on my own."

He lifted sad eyes to her. "You'll be fine. You were smart enough to get food and water, it must only be a matter of time before the Southern Ocean Patrol gets here. Just stay out of sight. You have the satellite phones, you can check in with Harris and let him know what's going on. I'll be all right, you'll be all right."

"I'm not buying that. You think they'll keep their word? They're *pirates*."

"I'm thinking it's a gesture of goodwill, and if I show myself and make it known to Harris where I am, this will be over. We'll all be safe."

She rolled her eyes. "That's never going to work."

"The other option is that they find us, and that will be less pleasant. I'm thinking if they have me, they'll be more merciful to the others." He curved his good hand around the back of her head and leaned forward to kiss her. His mouth was hot and she tasted a touch of desperation. He pulled away before she could lift her hands to grip his shoulders, holding him to her. He stroked her hair and let his hand fall away. "You'll be fine." He moved toward the opening of the vent.

"Where are you going?"

"If I waltz in through the kitchen door, they'll know where you're hiding. Even if they don't know you're here, I don't want them looking, you know?"

Smart. She nodded, even though every ounce of her being wanted to go with him, take her chances with the pirates. Instead, she sat on top of the freezer and watched Marcus disappear into the vent.

She couldn't bear not knowing what was going on, so slipped into the freezer, then into the kitchen, and crept over to the door to watch what would happen when Marcus entered.

***

Marcus had been called a hero before, a hero to kids who wanted to learn about snowboarding, to kids who liked sports. But he'd never acted heroically, and this was why. Being that guy was damned hard. His heart thundered as he climbed down from the vent into the hallway outside Brylie's room, where he'd entered the thing in the first place. Damn, he hadn't thought walking away from her would be so difficult, and the challenge was more than because he wanted to look out for her. It was knowing she had his back, knowing that he could trust her. He didn't remember the last time he trusted a woman, or even got to know one. Would he have spent the time getting to know Brylie if they hadn't been forced together?

Yeah, so he was no hero as he approached the doors to the dining room. He wanted to bolt, to say to hell with it all, but he had a responsibility here, and he didn't want anyone else hurt.

He pressed his good hand to the door only to have the barrier yanked inward. Someone grabbed his arm and dragged him through so that his first impressions of the room were jumbled—angry faces, terrified faces, overturned chairs, a body on the floor with the doctor kneeling beside it, her own face drawn with stress. Blood soaked the kid's shirt, the top of his jeans. Oh, hell. Not good. Even if the helicopter evacuated him, his chances were grim. But the doctor didn't stop.

Marcus landed on his knees with enough force to jar his teeth, and a blow to the back of his head made his eyes spin in their sockets. Yeah, this hero crap wasn't what it was cracked up to be. He looked up into the dark eyes of who he presumed was Hilario—at least the guy acted like he was leading this thing.

"You don't look like so much." Hilario jabbed a finger at his shoulder, the borrowed sweatshirt. "You are the one who killed one of my men?"

Marcus lifted his chin. "I think that was you. Threw him overboard, didn't you?"

Hilario's nostrils flared and Marcus realized he'd let Hilario know that he knew what was going on. Would the man figure out he'd been listening in? Marcus wasn't sure if that was good or bad. Probably would have been better to hold onto that information. Hell.

Hilario held out a hand behind him, and one of his men placed a sat phone in it. Hilario offered the phone to

Marcus. "You need to let your brother know you are with us, and if we don't receive the ransom money within the next four hours, we're going to start cutting off your fingers."

Fear bubbled up and escaped in a laugh. He curled his fingers inward and told himself it was to resist taking the phone, not to protect his fingers. "Yeah, well, Harris'll tell you I don't use my fingers all that much. Now my toes, I need them to snowboard. Otherwise, no balance, see."

Hilario's face twisted and he lifted his other hand as if to strike, then lowered it again and a smile curled his lips, though it didn't reach his flat dark eyes. "We can start with a different body part, if you prefer. I'm sure your brother will be horrified to receive that reminder that we are serious."

Marcus inclined his head, determined not to flinch. "Now that, he'll tell you I use too often. How will you be sending this? You have a courier service I don't know about?"

"We have ways."

Marcus damn near expected to see Hilario twirl an invisible moustache. He scanned the passengers who huddled together on the floor on the other side of the room, looking stunned and beaten, the douche among them, blending in. So they didn't know a traitor was among them. More than one—who was the other?

Hilario pressed a few buttons, then shoved the phone against Marcus's ear. "Tell your brother where you are and what I've said."

Marcus held Hilario's gaze as he spoke into the phone. "Harris. You may have heard I'm on a cruise in the Antarctic."

"I hear it's not going so well."

Leave it to Harris to match his smart-ass comment. He could picture his big brother in the Sydney office, sitting behind his desk, sleeves rolled up, hair rumpled as he worked through a solution. "No, the situation has deteriorated."

"They've taken you."

Pride wouldn't let him leave that one alone. "I wouldn't say taken so much as I surrendered. Two of the passengers aren't faring so well, from what I've seen. It was this or they'd drop them in the ocean."

"Shit. How many? Do you know now?"

Marcus was working out how to let his brother know that some of the passengers, and maybe employees, were in on it as well, when the phone was snatched from him.

"You believe me now that your brother is in my custody and in danger. You need to send the ransom now, to the coordinates I've given you. I'll be sending a man for the money at that time."

What was to stop Harris from sending cops with the money, or to just giving the coordinates to the authorities? Marcus wanted to ask the questions but didn't. He wanted to know if Brylie had called to let Harris know what was going on, how far out the Southern Ocean Patrol was. Now he had to wait with the others, wait and hope.

Two of Hilario's men yanked him to his feet and half-walked, half-dragged him across the room to the wall by the kitchen where the others were gathered.

The kitchen, where Brylie waited, safe.

Marcus looked at the other passengers. The douche was there, Trinity, her family, the other two adventurers, looking more shell-shocked than the rest. One kept his gaze riveted on his friend, the other anywhere else.

"Where's the captain?" Marcus asked Trinity, but she just shook her head and eased away. Poor kid.

"He's alive, isn't he?" he asked the adventurer, Evan, who wouldn't look at his friend.

The young man nodded, but wouldn't meet his gaze.

"Have they hurt anyone else?" he asked.

"Sh!" Trinity's mother hissed, folding her arms about her daughter, protecting the girl from his brashness and apparent inability to follow directions.

He folded his arms over his bent knees. "Right. So we just wait here and do as they say."

"If we don't like bleeding," the douche, who Marcus noticed wasn't bleeding, said.

"Quiet!" one of the pirates ordered.

Marcus squared his shoulders. He considered countering the order, but he could imagine Hilario taking out Marcus's punishment on one of the other passengers. So he kept his mouth shut.

***

He'd been sitting for a bit, trying not to think about his throbbing hand, easy enough to do when a kid was bleeding to death in front of him, when someone eased up behind him. He glanced back to see Monica, Brylie's assistant chef, the one who'd been so brave about getting the food for the other passengers, for taking Brylie's place.

"Is she okay?" Monica whispered, her voice barely audible.

He nodded. "She's safe."

"Alone now, though."

"With a phone and a gun, well-hidden."

Monica squeezed his arm in gratitude. He glanced about to gauge the distance of the other passengers, the interest they showed in his conversation with Monica, then leaned back a bit.

"Who is working with them?"

Monica's dark eyes widened. "What are you talking about?"

"Two passengers are helping them out—at least two. I know who one is, but can't figure out the voice of the other."

She leaned closer. "You heard them? Man or woman?"

"Man. Have you seen them go off with one of the passengers? Or maybe one of the crew?"

She shook her head, her full lips pressed together.

How could she not? Marcus had clearly heard the man and one of the pirates speaking in the kitchen. They had to have walked right past here. Of course, maybe Monica and the others were too shocked from the shooting to see anything else going on.

"What happened there?" He gestured with his head to the young man losing his battle despite the doctor's best efforts.

Monica glanced about and scooted closer. "After the storm, a couple of the pirates were ill. A few more were elsewhere on the ship, and only three remained in here. Those four guys were whispering together and they charged them at the same time. One of them was shot in the chest, and died right away. The other one was shot in the abdomen, and the other two were hit on the head and subdued."

"Was anyone else hurt?" Marcus had looked over the passengers, but didn't know if anyone was missing. But he had thought more people were on board to begin with.

"One of the tour guides was grazed." Monica nodded in the direction of a woman who cradled a bandaged arm.

"So where is everyone else?"

Monica shook her head. "This is everyone else."

He frowned. The roster had said two hundred people were on board, and another thirty as crew. He'd counted less than half of that in this room. The captain, he was sure, was on the bridge, and maybe a couple of others were running the ship. Had some been moved to the terrorists' ship?

"You!" One of the pirates, the one Marcus had heard called Israel, jabbed a finger in his direction. "It's time to feed these people."

Marcus braced his good hand on the carpet beneath him to rise, but Monica's grip on his shoulder told him she was the object of Israel's attention.

"I can help," he volunteered. He'd be in the kitchen, where Brylie was. He couldn't even glance at the freezer lest he give himself away, but just being closer to her would make him feel better.

Israel scowled. Marcus figured the kid couldn't be more than twenty. What was he doing with this bunch?

"You stay here, where we can keep an eye on you," Israel said, affecting a deep voice. "Those are my orders, so those are your orders." The young man scanned the crowd and his gaze landed on Trinity. "You. Help."

Trinity's mama opened her mouth to protest, but Trinity silenced her with a hand on her cheek. "I can help. Besides, the more help, the sooner we eat." She forced a smile and pushed to her feet.

Marcus felt an inexplicable sense of pride at Trinity's resilience. He'd been afraid when he'd first entered the room and found her cowering. He smiled at her when she passed, but she didn't acknowledge him.

Half an hour later, they sat on the floor eating sandwiches. Time was passing so slowly. Was the ransom on its way? Would Harris have been able to assemble it in that amount of time? How much time remained? There was no clock in the dining room and since the raid had happened at dawn, Marcus didn't see anyone other than one of the adventurers, Michael, wearing a watch, and he was across the room. Getting up to go talk to him didn't seem like such a great idea.

Hilario was in and out of the dining room, but always alone. Marcus watched to see if he gave special attention to any of the passengers, but the only one he seemed interested in was Trinity. Ah, hell. He knew that look. He might have to play hero after all.

***

The second man wasn't doing well. From where he sat, Marcus could see the young doctor Joan trembling with fatigue from her efforts. She had an assistant, but wouldn't allow herself to take a break. Marcus raised his hand to draw Israel's attention.

The young man jutted his chin at Marcus. "What do you want?"

"I want to help her. She's running out of gas." The young man frowned, clearly not understanding the term, so Marcus rephrased. "She's getting tired."

"And you have medical training?" Israel demanded.

"No, but I can do what she tells me to do." It would beat the hell out of sitting here helplessly.

Israel turned to Joan. "You want this man's help?"

She swiped the back of her hand across her cheek and looked from Israel to Marcus. "I could use a strong hand, and a strong stomach."

"Gut of iron," Marcus assured her, pressing his good hand on the carpet to push to his feet. He didn't want to mention his injury, didn't want Hilario or his men to know he had a weakness.

"One moment. I need to ask Hilario," Israel said, holding a hand out.

"What for?" Marcus stood, and realized he was half a head taller than the kid. That didn't happen often, so he used his size, moving closer and looking down his nose. "I'm just going on the other side of the room. I won't even hold the scissors if you don't want me to." He inclined his head. "Did you shoot him, Israel? Do you want him to die? Do you want that on your conscience?"

"No, I—" The boy stepped back, clearing Marcus's path to the injured young man.

He knelt across from Joan. "I'm Marcus."

She gave him a tired smile. "I remember."

"What's his name?"

"Jimmy."

Jimmy. A kid's name. He looked into Jimmy's slack, unconscious face and saw a young man of maybe twenty-five, a young man who thought he was invincible. Yeah, Marcus knew that feeling.

"Tell me what you want me to do." Keeping his voice low, he held out his injured hand. "I did some damage here, so I'm probably not as good to you as I made out to be."

"I'll take care of it in a few."

"No, I don't want them to know. Work with me, okay?"

She gave him a long look, then nodded and turned her attention back to Jimmy. They worked side by side, Marcus following her instructions. Even untrained, he could feel that Jimmy's pulse was thready, his breathing too shallow. Joan said something about sepsis and packing the wound, which she let Marcus do, taking wadded up gauze and sticking it into the hole in the kid's gut. What had they shot him with, a cannon?

"How much time has he got?" he asked quietly.

"Not enough," Joan said grimly.

Yeah, the, what, three hours now until the ransom got here, then a four-hour flight back? The kid was bleeding out.

Israel approached and looked over Marcus's shoulder. Marcus twisted his head and eyed the .45 in disgust. "Those things do a hell of a lot of damage. You better hope you're not on the receiving end one day."

The young man blanched and moved away. Marcus waited until Israel was out of earshot before he posed the same questions to Joan that he'd asked Monica. Of course Joan had been too busy with her patient to see if the terrorists had any special contact with any of the passengers, but Marcus wanted her to be aware.

"Take a break. There's nothing else you can do now, is there?"

She didn't take her gaze from the kid on the floor. "If anything goes wrong—"

"You'll be right over there. I'll call you."

She hesitated.

"I need your eyes. See what you can see." He shifted his gaze toward Hilario, who had just walked in.

"Marcus Devlin, you are a man of many talents." Hilario approached and kicked Jimmy's foot, not even eliciting a groan from the patient.

"Most people say I just have a short attention span. Can't sit still long."

"Which makes me wonder what trouble you got into before you walked into this room. And who you got into it with."

Marcus's blood chilled. Did they know about Brylie? Had the douche or his accomplice remembered seeing Marcus and Brylie together, and mentioned that to Hilario?

"I get in plenty of trouble all by myself, mate. You can ask Harris if you don't believe me."

"Oh, I do believe you. I do. But there's the case of the missing chef."

He hoped his face was expressionless as he thought. "I thought Monica was the chef."

"The redhead. A real beauty from what I understand. And one you gave special attention to."

Fuck. Douchebag had spoken. "I never forget a pretty face, but I don't remember a redhead on this cruise. But I'm partial to brunettes, myself."

Quick as a snake, Hilario whipped out his gun and pressed the barrel to the top of Marcus's thigh. Marcus struggled not to swallow, not to show fear as Hilario squeezed the back of his neck at the same time.

"Where is she?"

"You shoot me there, and I'll be dead as this guy," Marcus pointed out. "Femoral artery, see? And a dead Devlin ain't going to win you any favors."

Hilario shifted the gun to the outside of Marcus's knee. Shit. He could do a hell of a lot of damage there. "Where is the chef?"

"Right over there." He pointed to Monica with a bloodstained hand. "She told you so herself. Look, have any of the people here seen a redhead?" He raised his voice to address the group.

They murmured their negative responses, shaking their heads. Marcus turned to look into Hilario's eyes, not daring to wipe the sweat beading on his upper lip. "You're mistaken, mate. No redhead here."

"When I find her," Hilario said, his voice a growl, "It will not go easy on her."

"Then it's a good thing she's a figment of your imagination. Now if you don't mind, I'm trying to save a life here."

Hilario leaned close. "You should be more concerned with your own life. And that of the redhead if I find her." He moved away before Marcus could respond.

Marcus was grateful his hand had been occupied pressing the gauze to Jimmy's wound, so Hilario hadn't been able to see how he was shaking. If Hilario decided to go looking for Brylie, would she be able to get away? Would she be able to fight back? She should be safe as long as she stayed on the freezer.

"Find her," Hilario told his men, striding from the room.

CHAPTER SIX

Brylie couldn't stand it a moment longer. Honestly, she was ready to turn herself in. Being a hostage had to beat hiding alone on top of a damn freezer. She had to know what was going on.

Careful to make sure the gun safety was on, she tucked it into her pants the way she'd seen Marcus do. She didn't think she could use it in any case, but just the weight of it made her feel safer. She would have to carry the sat phone, though, since it was too big for her pockets. That would make crawling through the vent tricky, but she didn't want to be without it. She was out of touch enough as it was.

She wasn't entirely sure where she was heading. The dining room didn't have a raised ceiling the way the lounge did, so she couldn't spy from the vent. Honestly, the thing she wanted most was to see the S.O.P. ship chugging toward them. She wanted that hope. She wanted this to be over.

After she hoisted herself into the vent, she made her way toward the stern. She didn't know exactly where the pirates' vessel was, but imagined it was beside the ship, not in front of it. Her best shot of not being seen was to exit at the bow or stern, and rescue was likely coming from behind. Plus, if she remembered right, there was a closed-in observation deck. If she was very careful, she could make that her nest for the next hour or so.

The vent didn't lead to the observation deck, so she hoped Hilario's crew was elsewhere as she climbed down into the hallway and crept along the wall to her goal.

Too late, she remembered the observation deck was accessible by key card and Marcus had told her that her key card no longer worked. Great. Now what was she going to do?

A solution would come to her. It had to. She wasn't turning back. She could jimmy the lock, except she had no idea how to do that. She could find another nest, which wouldn't be easy with no key card.

Damn it, she needed to get in there. She drew the gun from the waistband, double-checked the safety, and rapped the butt of the gun against the glass, close to the handle. The vibration sent terror through her—how far could someone feel that? She looked over her shoulder and struck it again, as hard as she could. One more time, and the glass cracked. A fourth time—careful not to be too rhythmic in her blows—and it broke. Cautiously she pushed the glass away and reached through to open the door. On the off chance the pirates would see the broken glass, she picked up the bigger pieces and tossed them in a nearby receptacle, then rubbed at the smaller pieces with her shoe, working them into the carpet. Then she closed the door behind her and found a chair that, if angled just right, would hide her from the doorway and allow her a view of the ship's wake.

She tucked the pistol and phone against her hip and curled up in the chair, letting the churning water below soothe her pounding pulse. She wished Marcus was here with her, or at least that she could be sure he was safe.

***

The boy Jimmy died. Marcus felt his life fade away under his hands, and never had he been so helpless in his life. Joan had scrambled over and worked heroically, but the kid had lost too much blood. He wouldn't have survived the trip to the mainland in any case, but that didn't make Marcus feel better. He stripped off the rubber gloves coated with the kid's blood, slumped against the wall and buried his face in his hands, doing his best to block out the sniffles and sobs from the other passengers.

What could he have done to prevent this? If he and Brylie hadn't hidden, would Jimmy be alive? Maybe, but maybe not. Marcus knew all about feeling invincible, and these guys had that in spades. They might have still attacked, Israel might still have panicked. Too bad the young terrorist was such a good shot.

He lifted his head and met Israel's gaze. "Let's get him out of here, all right?"

"I need to ask—"

"Screw that." Marcus got to his feet in one movement. "We need him out of here before everyone gets more worked up. You can help me, or she can." He pointed to Joan, who wouldn't look at him as she repacked her medical supplies. Her movements were shaky with weariness. He hated the thought that she could rest now that Jimmy was dead. He turned back to Israel. "You take his feet, I'll take his shoulders. We'll put him in the next room with his friend."

Israel hesitated and Marcus crossed to him, though his pulse skipped when Israel raised his gun in his direction.

"Are you going to shoot me, too?" He lowered his voice. "No one wants to be in here with a body. Just give them that much peace."

Israel's mouth twisted, but he nodded, motioning for Marcus to take Jimmy's shoulders. Marcus nodded and bent, maneuvering to hook one wrist under one armpit, gripping the other. Jimmy was muscular—no wonder he thought he was invincible. Marcus couldn't look at the others, at Jimmy's friends, as he lifted the boy. Joan scrambled to her feet and hurried to open the door. She cast Marcus a grateful glance as he passed by her, doing his damnedest not to think about his burden, about the pain shooting up his arm from his injured hand. He backed into the room and approached the other body, covered with a blanket, and placed Jimmy carefully beside him, watching Israel do the same.

The terrorist's gun hung at an angle from his hip. Marcus couldn't let himself think about the consequences. He needed to do this. Sweeping his injured arm up, he shoved the young pirate across the bodies, using his forearm as he grabbed for the gun with his good hand. He yanked it free from Israel's belt, slid off the safety in one fluid movement and pointed it at the kid's chest. Fear flashed in the boy's eyes, but Marcus couldn't let himself think about that.

"I want to know how many of you there are, and who from this ship is working with you."

Israel didn't speak, only raised his hands in surrender. Marcus backed toward the door to ensure no other pirates were coming through, and saw Joan standing guard. Tough lady. How she'd known what he was going to do when even he hadn't known...still, he was grateful for her foresight.

He crossed back to Israel, motioning with the pistol. "Tell me."

"You won't shoot me," Israel said, pulling himself to a sitting position, off of the bodies. "They'll hear you and come."

"No?" Marcus angled his head, hating that the boy was right. "But I can do this." He swung the barrel of the gun as hard as he could against Israel's knee.

The boy howled, but stopped the sound when Marcus brought the barrel up to point at his throat, careful to keep it out of Israel's reach.

"There are other sensitive places I can damage. Tell me what I want to know. How many, and who is working with you? And where are the other hostages?"

"Fifteen, including the crew on our ship. And I don't know the names of the people helping. One is a big, angry man with dark thinning hair."

The douche.

"The other is short, young, *fuerte*."

Marcus had enough Spanish to know that meant "strong."

"Is he in there now?" He motioned to the dining room.

Israel shook his head. "He's on the other ship."

"Your ship. The ship you came on? With the other hostages?"

Israel nodded frantically. Marcus backed away, lowering the pistol to his side. He saw the shift of Israel's eyes too late, and the blow to the back of his head dropped him like a rock.

***

Brylie leaned forward in her chair. Was that—it was hard to see at this distance, but it looked like a ship on the horizon. She held her breath—as if that could help her see better—and wished she had binoculars.

Please be them, oh, please let this be over.

As she strained to see, the spot grew larger, but still she worried it was part of her imagination. She didn't allow herself to believe until the ship was a few hundred yards out, and then she used all her self-control not to jump up and down and squeal with glee. She picked up the sat phone and dialed Harris's direct line. When she'd first spoken to him after Marcus surrendered, his voice had sounded so like Marcus's that she trusted him immediately. He'd cursed his brother's impulse to put himself in danger, though hadn't been surprised by it.

"Harris, they're here—the Southern Ocean Patrol is approaching. It's going to be over soon."

No longer concerned about being seen, not with rescue so close at hand, she rose to watch the approach.

"There she is!"

She heard the shout behind her, turned to see two men running down the hallway toward her. Panic slammed through her, chasing hope. She was trapped, no escape, and the other ship was still hundreds of yards away. She turned to look at it, as if she could will it to move closer, to rescue her.

A whistling sound from the port side of the Ice Queen grabbed her attention and she saw something spiraling through the air. She realized what it was the moment before it struck the S.O.P. vessel, sending a fireball through the middle of it, splitting it in two. The men on board dove for the lifeboats, knowing they'd never survive in the frigid water.

"Oh, my God, oh, my God."

She was vaguely aware of Harris shouting at her through the phone, demanding to know what was going on, but she dropped it to the chair beside the gun. Horror raced through her at what she'd just seen, anger chasing it, an anger stronger than she'd ever felt. She picked up the pistol, flicked off the safety and turned to face her pursuers.

***

Marcus woke in a dark room with a throbbing headache. He lifted his hand to the knot on the back of his head and felt the crustiness of dried blood. Probing further, he encountered the gash just above the base of his neck. Yeah, that was going to leave a mark.

He squinted against the darkness but he couldn't see anything. So it wasn't a matter of adjusting to the light—he was in a black-as-pitch room. He was alone. He could sense that much. How long? What time was it now?

He reached out with a foot to find the floor, sat up and gripped the edge of the bunk. Okay, so a cabin. But his head throbbed and spun, and he squeezed his eyes shut even though he couldn't see anything. Weird how it seemed to help. He wanted to lie back down on the bunk until the dizziness passed. But Brylie was out there. Was she safe?

He pushed to his feet, bracing his hands on the edge of the bed for a moment before he lurched toward the door. Locked, of course, which made him wonder what kind of room this was that they could lock from the outside. Maybe just jammed. He tugged on the handle, then realizing he didn't really need to be quiet, he jostled it harder, pounding on the door. Let them think he was panicking, he didn't care.

He felt along the wall for a switch, trying to remember where the one in his room had been located. When he finally found the knob and flicked it, nothing happened. They'd disconnected the light somehow when he'd been out.

The thin door rattled under his fist, and the handle seemed to be looser. He wished he could see, maybe find a tool. He felt his way back to the wall, a hand out in search of a curtain drawn over a window, but he only encountered solid wall.

An interior room—a crew member's room, probably, since the cruise advertised that every room had a view. The crew member that he suspected? He ran his hands over the bunk to the drawers underneath. But even if he found something there, he couldn't see it. He straightened and braced his good hand on the bed in front of him. What now? Was he a prisoner until the ransom arrived? And was Brylie safe?

***

The first shot went wild as the gun bucked in her hand. Brylie braced her right hand under her left and fired again, three more times. The first man fell on her second shot, the second man took two. She kept the gun trained in front of her as she approached the men on the hallway floor, where they groaned and clutched their wounded legs. She just hadn't been able to bring herself to shoot them in the chest, shoot to kill.

One of their guns had fallen in her direction and she crouched to retrieve it. She wanted the other gun, too, and at least one radio, but was wary of getting too close. Even now she risked too much—the man whose gun was still tucked away, the man with two bullets in him, could draw it and shoot her.

Her attention on them, she tucked the stolen gun in her pants and backed away. She snatched the phone from the chair and ran. No doubt Hilario had heard the shots and would send more men after her. She didn't know where she was going to go, but she couldn't stay here. She started to tuck her gun away, but the barrel was hot from being fired—why didn't they ever tell you that on the cop shows? So she carried it in one hand, the phone—with Harris squawking—in the other, and refusing to look at the carnage on the sea, headed back down to the second level. She needed to find Marcus.

CHAPTER SEVEN

Brylie trembled as she stood outside the bridge. She wasn't quite tall enough to see through the window set in the door, not without putting herself off balance. She didn't know for certain if her father was in there, but if the pirates were smart, they'd have him piloting his ship through these waters. And she'd given her approach a lot of consideration. She wouldn't have exposed herself except that the crew from the Southern Ocean Patrol needed help. So she'd come to rescue her father.

She only wished she knew who else was in there with him.

Entry to the bridge was not easy—both doors were clearly visible from any part of the room. She'd have to go in low, assess quickly and not hesitate. She just couldn't think about what she was doing when she fired her weapon. She turned the door handle slowly, crouching so she'd be hidden behind the console when she entered, on the off chance no one saw the door opened. Also, if bullets started flying, she had something to hide behind. Wouldn't be good for the running of the ship, but...

Taking a deep breath, she pushed the door inward and waited for the shout of alarm, but it didn't come. She slipped through the narrow opening on trembling legs and pushed the door closed so it wouldn't slam. So far, so good. No sense pushing her luck. Listening for voices to give her the locations of the terrorists and crew, she crept to the far side of the room, but no one spoke. She was going to have to chance a peek.

Cursing her red hair, she rose slowly and peered over the edge of the console. Her father stood at the bridge, and her heart kicked in relief. He was safe. But before she could see which of his crew members were present, a shout directly across from her drew her attention. One of the pirates had spotted her, and though she didn't see him holding a gun, she raised hers in both hands and fired, striking him in the shoulder, sending him staggering. Another shot cracked the glass behind him.

Shit. Wasted bullet, and now he was out of sight. Everyone had ducked down when she fired, so she still didn't know how many friends or how many enemies were on the bridge.

The window beside her head splintered before she registered the sound of the gun firing, and she dropped to the floor, blood surging. A few inches to the right and she'd be dead. She couldn't die in front of her father.

Suddenly the man himself was beside her and took the gun from her with his big, competent hands. He rose on one knee and fired measured shots over the console until he was empty, then swore.

"Ammo?" he demanded.

She shook her head but shoved the other gun at him, with no idea how many bullets it contained.

"Stay down," he ordered, and repeated the attack. Behind him, the cracked window shattered, and icy air flowed into the room.

A movement from the corner of her eye drew her attention as one of the pirates crept around the end of the console. Someone who'd been in here the whole time, or had someone come to investigate the shooting? She hadn't thought to secure the door against more intruders.

When the pirate raised his pistol to fire at her father, she launched herself at the terrorist with a cry, hitting him mid-body, below his gun arm. The weapon fired, and she prayed the shot went wild as her momentum slammed the guy against the wall. She grasped his arm and twisted with all her strength. Surprise worked to her advantage, and the gun dropped to the deck with a thud. Both of them scrambled for it. She felt the roughness of the grip beneath her fingertips before it was snatched away, but she didn't give up. To do that meant she and her father would die.

A deafening shot behind her had the man she fought with bucking, then going limp. She looked up to see blood pouring from a hole in his head, his eyes glazed over, sightless. She grabbed the gun from his slack hand and scrambled back to her father.

"How many?" she asked.

"There were three."

"Was he one?"

Her father looked over. "Yeah."

"I'm going to secure the door."

He made a sound of protest, but she didn't look over her shoulder, instead stepping over the dead man on her way to the main entrance. She was shaking by the time she reached it, and her ears rang so badly from the gunfire that a moment passed before she realized there had been no more gunshots.

"Mac?" her father called.

"Got 'im," the bosun replied.

"Carl?"

"Yeah, he's down."

"Brylie?"

"I've got the door." She straightened to see him crossing the room to her, his expression an odd mixture of fury and relief. He gripped her shoulders, one hand still holding the pistol, and glared at her.

"What were you thinking coming in here?"

"I was thinking you need control of the ship!" she retorted. "And now we can get those men out of the water."

Pain flickered in his eyes, letting her know he'd seen what she had. "Where did you get the guns?"

"Marcus got one from someone when he came in to steal the satellite phone and make the distress call. I got the other—just now."

"Just found it lying about, did you?"

She couldn't meet his gaze and tell him the truth. "No."

"Christ, Brylie." He pulled her against his massive chest and curved his big hand over the back of her head.

She gave in to the comfort he offered—just for a moment before she stepped back. "We need to help those men now. Turn the ship."

His mouth tightened. "I can't. We're tethered to the pirates' ship.

"The zodiacs—Mac, Carl and I can take them out."

Her father's face reddened. "And get blown out of the water as well? We may have control of the bridge, but not the ship. These men are far better armed than we are."

"I expect them to come charging in here any minute," Mac said, moving toward the door.

As if to affirm his prediction, one of the radios on one of the fallen men squawked. Sharp Spanish commands poured out. Not Hilario's voice, but someone demanded to know what was going on, demanded a report. Brylie wanted to grab the radio, but didn't want to get close enough to the man who wore it, just in case he was still alive, still strong enough to fight back.

Cal didn't have the same qualms. He walked over, kicked the man in the head so that it lolled to the other side, and yanked the radio off his belt. He lifted the radio to his lips and pressed the button. Brylie held her breath, knowing Cal's hot head didn't always think things through. But before he could speak, her father crossed the bridge and held out a hand. Cal handed over the radio and her father turned it down.

Her father was right, of course. They wouldn't be able to help the men from the S.O.P. until they could get away from the pirate ship. And they couldn't get away from the pirate ship unless they fought back.

There were four of them, now, and three fewer pirates. Five, counting the two she shot on her way here.

But they were still outnumbered, and the terrorists had the hostages as collateral. Including Marcus. Helplessness swamped her and she dropped to the floor.

"You can't stay here," her father said. "They'll be here any moment and I don't want you caught in the line of fire."

She opened her mouth to protest that they all needed to get out. But her father couldn't leave the bridge. What they needed was to be better armed, and Marcus had hidden an automatic weapon. She didn't know how to use it, but maybe Carl did. She pushed to her feet, using the wall behind her to brace herself.

"All right. But I want Carl to come with me. Mac can stay here and watch your back. Is your key card still working?"

Both crewmen turned to their captain with raised eyebrows. Her father frowned at her, knowing there was something she wasn't telling him, before he nodded gruffly and drew out the key card. "I can reactivate it now. Give me a minute."

With an ear tuned to hear gunfire from either the bridge or the dining room, she retraced Marcus's steps. The weapon was in the fourth linen closet she checked, much to Carl's annoyance.

"Hey, we haven't heard anyone moving around yet," she said as she handed him the weapon, which he checked like a pro.

"That's what has me worried." He tucked the weapon under his arm.

"Take that back to the bridge." She closed the door, pocketed the key card and turned toward the dining room.

"And where are you going, missy?"

"I need to go get Marcus."

***

Brylie went over the layout of the ship for the thousandth time since the pirates boarded. She knew of only one way to look into the dining room, to see if Marcus was in there, and how many terrorists remained. She had to get into her kitchen and look through the doors—and hope no one decided at that point to get hungry.

Now, how she'd get Marcus away without being noticed was a whole other problem. But she needed his help, or the men in the water would die.

She pressed the swinging door open as slightly as she could manage. Three men with guns stood over the passengers, who were seated on the floor, their backs to the wall separating dining room and kitchen, which made it difficult to see their faces. Damn it.

Before she could think of what to do, someone rose and moved toward the kitchen, followed by one of the guards. She hadn't heard anything said, or seen a signal. What was going on? Was this the other person helping the terrorists?

But no, it was Monica. Brylie ducked out of the doorway, considered briefly, then slipped into the pantry. This way, she might have a chance to talk to Monica, and see where Marcus was.

She hoped Monica was a good actress.

Monica shoved through the door with more force than necessary, nearly beaning the young guard who followed her when the door made its return swing. He cursed as Monica crossed the room, stopping at the counter just to the right of the pantry, in Brylie's line of sight. Brylie sucked in a breath, wondering if she should say something now. But no, Monica would get scared, her guard would notice, and she'd be caught. She'd wait until Monica stepped into the pantry.

Please let Monica come into the pantry.

Monica moved out of view, then back in, assembling more sandwiches. When it looked like she'd skip the pantry altogether, Brylie reached back and crinkled a bag of chips on the shelf. Monica's head shot up, and she met Brylie's gaze through the door. Brylie jerked her head to motion for Monica to come inside. Monica glanced over her shoulder to see where the guard was, and muttered something about needing more mustard, before she slipped into the pantry. She pulled the door closed behind her.

The women embraced—Brylie didn't want to let go. Her friend was shaking all over.

"Are you okay?" Brylie asked.

"I'm fine!" Monica eased back and braced a hand on her hip, her gaze searching Brylie's face. "What about you?"

Brylie waved the question away. "What's going on in there? Who's in there? Is Marcus?"

Monica shook her head. "No, he tried to take out one of the guards, so they took him away. I heard him shouting down the hall. I think he's in one of the crew's cabins."

The door handle jiggled and Monica smacked her hand over it. "I'll *be* right there." She turned back to Brylie. "What are you going to do?"

"I'm going to get him. We're getting you out of this, I promise." She squeezed her friend's hand. "You'd better go."

"How are you going to get there?"

"I'll figure it out. Go, before he gets suspicious."

Monica nodded once, and turned away, pulling the door closed behind her. Brylie waited a few minutes before creeping into the freezer to get back in the vent.

There was no direct way from the vent to the hallway with the crew cabins—her cabin wasn't in that hallway. She had to crawl to the perpendicular hallway, lower herself into the open, and creep back down the hall.

She didn't have to worry too much about making noise, because he was making enough for ten people. At least she knew where he was. No one stood guard in front of Marcus's room, but how were they keeping him inside? She approached the door and tried the key card, but while the light flashed green, the handle didn't respond. He rattled the door, so the handle must somehow be disabled from this side. She couldn't see what was holding it in place, but she was running out of time and couldn't spend the time to figure it out. She stepped away from the door and kicked the handle as hard as she could. Marcus shouted in alarm from the other side of the door, but she didn't want to take the time or the energy to explain. She kicked again. And again. And felt the handle give.

Just when she raised her leg to kick one more time, the door dragged inward and Marcus surged into the opening.

"What the—?" Then he saw her, leaned against the jamb and grinned. "Come to rescue me?"

She frowned and looked up and down the hall before shoving the other gun at him. "They've shot the S.O.P. out of the water. My father has control of the bridge but we can't maneuver to help the survivors with the other ship tethered to us. We need to break free of it."

His expression sobered immediately as he palmed the weapon. "Are you all right?"

She couldn't meet his gaze because if she did, she'd burst into tears. She couldn't stop to think about what she'd done over the past few hours. Even now she was shaking with exhaustion. But she couldn't rest until those men were out of the water and everyone was safe. She nodded.

"We have to get loose from the pirate ship."

"How are we doing that, exactly?" He scanned the hall, then curved his hand around her upper arm and drew her with him in the direction away from the dining room.

"Remember those water cannons my father told us about earlier on the cruise? You're going to man one while I remove the lines between the ships."

"The hell you are."

She should have known he'd argue with her. "I can do it quickly. I'm not strong enough to use a cannon. And we don't know if anyone will see us."

"We're not dressed to go out in the weather, much less get wet."

"We'll go by and pick up slickers. We have to do this, Marcus. Those men have been exposed too long already. They were coming to save us. We owe them."

He grunted his agreement and let her take the lead.

"You got the key card to work?" he asked when she slid it into a slot in the door.

"My dad reactivated his once we had control of the bridge." She opened the door to reveal a room full of galoshes and yellow slickers.

"Maybe dressing in yellow isn't the best way to avoid notice," he murmured, slipping past her to select a coat, checking the lining. Also yellow.

"It's in case we're washed over the side, easier to spot in the water."

He snapped his head around to stare at her. She shrugged into a coat of her own and buckled it up.

"There's no one to rescue us, so don't fall in."

The initial danger, as she saw it, was that someone from the pirate's vessel would spot them before she could show Marcus how to operate the high-pressure hose. He was right about the yellow jackets. But otherwise, they'd freeze in the spray. She looked through the window, saw no one on the opposite deck, and opened the door.

The wind took her breath, blowing cold against her exposed face, and her first thought was to retreat. But if she was this cold, those men in the water—even the ones who'd made it to the life boats—were in worse shape. And she and Marcus were the only ones who could help.

She took his hand and felt him tense as she led him to the water cannon. She unlocked it, aimed it toward the other ship and showed him how to fire it, and how to pivot it on the fulcrum. When he nodded, his gaze riveted to the pirate vessel, she dashed across the deck to the first grappling line.

***

Marcus gripped the controls of the metal water cannon, ready to spin it either at their own ship or the enemy's. All he wanted to do was watch Brylie's progress as he moved from one line to the next. He hadn't seen how many there were, but he counted off as she moved down the deck, keeping her in his peripheral vision, easy enough to do with that damned yellow coat.

Jesus, it was freezing out here, and though he'd grabbed gloves and boots in the supply room, the wind cut right through. He wanted to get Brylie back inside, huddle up with her on the freezer, hold her tight, keep her safe.

But they couldn't wait on rescue anymore. They had to be their own rescue. He wondered if she'd be so brave if she'd seen what they did to Jimmy.

He realized then she'd lingered too long in one place. He took his attention from the pirate vessel just long enough to see her hunched down, over a tangled line. Christ. He didn't have a knife. Had she thought to get one? Every minute she was at the rail, she was vulnerable, and he had no faith in this cannon being able to protect her if someone walked out with a gun.

Finally, she was moving on and just as he breathed a sigh of relief, a door on the other ship opened. He opened his mouth to shout at her but she saw, too, and ducked below the rail. But too late.

The pirate gave a shout of alarm and raised his weapon. Marcus pulled the trigger. The stream of water slammed him back against the side of the ship, knocking his gun free. But instead of running to safety, Brylie ran to the next rope. *Shit.* He couldn't watch her when the other terrorists could be coming out at any moment, from either side. He could only be ready and pray he could keep her safe.

He sure as hell wasn't cold any longer as adrenaline poured through him. Shouts echoed behind him. *Christ, Brylie, leave it. Leave it!* But he couldn't shout, couldn't distract her, distract himself. His shoulders felt like they were going to snap as she loosened the last rope and tossed it over the side. She pivoted toward him and raced toward him, just as the door at the other end of the Ice Queen opened and two men ran out.

Marcus made the call—he abandoned the water cannon and shoved open the door they'd come out. Brylie raced as gunfire rang out, and dove through the door. Marcus started to follow her, then jerked back as a bullet impacted the door inches from his face. Holy hell.

If he didn't move now, he'd be stuck, and God knew what they'd do to him. So he crouched low and followed Brylie inside, praying the pirates' aim would be off as they ran.

He hit the floor at Brylie's feet and pulled the door closed behind him. "Get me something to jam the door." The door had been thick enough to stop the bullet at a distance, but up close—he didn't think so. They needed to get out of this hallway.

She made a complete circle before she disappeared into the supply room and returned with what looked like a harpoon. Whatever. He snatched it from her and wedged it crossways against the door, then grabbed her hand and bolted down the hallway as the first bullets slammed into the door.

"The bridge," she managed to gasp. "We need to let my father know we can go back!"

Though the action grated against every instinct of self-preservation, he headed toward the bridge. Christ, her hand was cold in his. She'd shed the gloves she'd been wearing, but her fingers were like ice. All he wanted was to take her into his arms and warm her up. Maybe once they were safely on the bridge.

They turned the corner and Marcus's heart kicked hard against his ribs. Two pirates forced the crew of three—her father, Carl and Mac—onto their knees, their hands folded behind their heads. Behind him, Brylie sucked in a hard breath, then swayed and grasped the wall beside her, her face pale. Marcus was torn between helping her and acting. He had seen that position in movies—the crew was going to be executed.

Marcus shoved her behind him. His muscles trembled as he raised his pistol. The report of the shots echoed off the thin walls. The terrorists lifted their weapons away from the crew and toward Marcus.

Shit. He took a step back, one arm out, as if that would shield Brylie. He should have left her somewhere else before he started shooting. They had no cover in the middle of the hallway. Before he could reason out what to do, Brylie stepped from behind Marcus, her pistol braced in both hands. She squeezed the trigger until only clicks were her response, and two bodies sprawled in front of her father, motionless.

"Christ, Brylie." Marcus stared at her as her father and his crew scrambled to retrieve the weapons from the fallen terrorists. She'd killed them, her face absolutely expressionless. Cold. It needed to be done, or they'd be dead, but he didn't want her to live with knowing she'd taken lives.

He was still staring at her when her father approached.

"I need more ammunition," Brylie told the captain.

"No. You don't." Marcus didn't want to see her shoot someone else, didn't want to see that hard look in her eyes. Her hands weren't even shaking, That would come later, though. And he wanted to be there when it did.

That realization terrified him as much as facing down two pistols.

Her father didn't seem to notice his daughter's demeanor, didn't seem to care that she'd killed two men. She'd saved his life, but…

Brylie followed her father, stiff-shouldered and stiff-gaited, onto the bridge. Marcus had no choice but to follow her. The room was frigid, for God's sake. No wonder. One of the windows was shattered and wind was blowing in. Marcus flexed the fingers of his good hand against the chill. The captain crossed to a closet near the door and drew out more heavy weather gear for Marcus and Brylie. This time the coats were weather-proofed and warm, lined with fleece, as were the gloves. Marcus felt marginally warmer, though he still fantasized about a hot bath. The captain led them onto the deck and pointed to a location where he needed them to help the injured and frightened men on board.

How the captain maneuvered the cruise ship as deftly as he did, Marcus had no idea. One of the other crew members stood guard with the automatic weapon—Hilario's remaining men would be on them in no time after hearing the firefight—but they couldn't hide, couldn't delay getting these men out of the water.

Many of the S.O.P crew had made it to the life rafts, though from where Marcus stood on the deck, he could see some stretched out on the bottom, either badly injured or badly frozen. They'd need to get Joan to help them, but she was still a hostage.

A terrible thought entered his head. What if Hilario started executing the hostages in retribution for the damage done to his team? That was something else Marcus would have to live with—the choices he'd made on this trip.

He couldn't think about that now, could only throw the rope ladders over the side and offer his good hand to help the men climb to safety. He'd ignore the bodies floating in the water, and wouldn't wonder what he could have done differently. Hilario's actions, not his.

Just his responsibility.

By the time the men were aboard—as many as they could find, dead and alive—one man emerged as the leader, a midshipman, Simon O'Loughlin. He moved across the deck, grim-faced, as he surveyed the survivors, every line in his body tense.

Marcus's gut twisted, a combination of sympathy for the crew of the S.O.P., and fear that the terrorists would attack at any minute. Hilario had to know they'd fished the crew out of the water, so where was he? Now would be the time to attack, when they were confused and vulnerable. They were racing time here, and everything seemed to be moving in slow motion. And yet, even as part-owner of the ship, he didn't have authority, not when the captain and the S.O.P. midshipman knew more about what to do next. Once again, he didn't have a place.

He glanced at Brylie, who was directing the men into the relative warmth of the bridge, her face flushed with the cold and exertion, though her expression hadn't changed since she killed those men in the hall. He wanted to take her hand, wanted to help her hold on to her humanity here. God, she'd been so soft and tender when he'd met her. He hated Hilario for changing her.

Once the men were indoors, crowded on the bridge and in the hall, Marcus could wait no longer. He squeezed past equipment and shivering men to reach the midshipman. "We need to get to the hostages. Hilario may use them as retribution for us helping you. He doesn't have a lot of men left, but they're all well-armed."

The man nodded, his lips pressed together, his gaze moving over his men. "The original plan is shot to shit," he said. "Most of my weapons went in the water. What have you got?"

The man's brow furrowed as Marcus and the captain laid out their cache on the console. "Not a lot to work with."

The comment didn't inspire a lot of confidence but these guys were trained, right? They went up against poachers, most often, though, not assholes holding people as collateral. Men who'd already killed two. Tension knotted Marcus's stomach as he watched the midshipman's face and waited. The need to move burned in every muscle, and this guy was taking his sweet time.

O'Loughlin stepped back. "I need to get an idea of the layout of the ship."

"You couldn't have done that on the way out here?" Marcus demanded.

O'Loughlin looked at him, his face unreadable. "I wasn't in charge of this mission."

"My daughter Brylie knows the ship," Captain Winston said. "Brylie. Show Mr. O'Loughlin the layout. I need to get the ship back on course."

She nodded briefly and crossed the room to pull out a shallow drawer. O'Loughlin followed with one of those military-man strides, and traced his finger over the blueprints of the ship. Was that what they were called? He followed, standing across from Brylie, more out of a sense of possession than the ability to offer more insight.

"How is it you escaped being a hostage?" O'Loughlin asked her.

Her cheeks pinkened. "Marcus thought quickly and got us into hiding. We were able to move about the ship and avoid detection for almost two days."

Marcus fought to ignore the rumble of jealousy in his gut, especially when the handsome older guy—tall dark and handsome, if you were into that—flashed Brylie a smile, and she returned it. He resisted the urge to reach across and lay a hand on her, stake a claim. He'd never wanted to do that before. But he could read the tension in her shoulders that made him think she'd rip his hand off. When this was over, he would…what? Tell her he loved her and wanted to live happily ever after? That was not his deal.

***

He cooled his heels and waited until they worked on the plan, their voices melding, a note of surprise in O'Loughlin's when Brylie offered a counter idea.

"We need to move now," Marcus broke in. "Hilario has to know most of his men are down. He doesn't have much to lose, and who knows how he'll respond to that?"

"Most of my men are down, too, and we have two ships to cover."

"So you're waiting for what? Back-up? It took you guys days to get here. We need to go."

O'Loughlin's lips pressed together. "Who are you, exactly?"

Marcus was aware of the pride that made him square his shoulders and draw himself to his full height—half a head shorter than this asshole. He was aware, and ashamed. Still, he said, "Marcus Devlin. Owner."

O'Loughlin's eyebrows went up, and he glanced from Marcus to Brylie, who blushed again. Then he nodded. He motioned to the men behind him who were fit enough, and he armed them with the weapons from the fallen terrorists.

When Brylie stood, Marcus stepped in front of her. "You stay here."

Her eyes flashed. "Why? Because I'm a girl?"

"Because you're a chef, not a counterterrorist agent."

Her hip shot out and her head went back in defiance. "I've shot four of them, Marcus, and came for you."

"Which is why I want you out of the line of fire." He couldn't explain to her now, not here with O'Loughlin listening, why this was important to him. He inclined his head in O'Loughlin's direction. "Let people who know what they're doing take care of it."

"I know this ship better than anyone here, outside of my father and his crew, and they have a job to do. You can feel free to stay behind."

"The hell I will." He wondered if this was how his family felt when he insisted on doing something idiotic. Looked like he was going to add to that list, because he sure as hell wasn't letting her out of his sight until this was over. He checked the ammunition in his own weapon—six bullets—and tucked it away. "Let's go."

***

Brylie was still seething at Marcus's high-handed attempt to get her to stay behind as they went to free the other hostages. She was damned tired of him trying to protect her when she'd proved herself more than capable of taking care of herself—and him. She hated that his desire to shelter her made her feel weak.

Still, her stomach heaved with the idea of shooting someone else, no matter what a terrible person he was. She'd watched bullets from her gun go into the bodies of four men, watched them fall. Adrenaline pushed her forward at the time, but God. She'd shot people. She remembered how Marcus had reacted after he shot the man on the bridge, how the guilt of the man's death had affected him. Of course. That was why he was looking out for her, trying to protect her. She shouldn't be so rough on him. When this was over, she'd apologize for giving him attitude.

When this was over…then what?

Simon and two of his men peeled away at her signal—they would board the pirate ship, free the hostages held there and ensure the terrorists couldn't make their escape. She hoped Hilario was on that ship, because she didn't want to face him.

She, Marcus and two of the S.O.P. team entered the kitchen and stood inside the swinging doors for a moment, weapons drawn. Marcus peeked through the small crack he made and held up three fingers, then signaled where they were in the room—one by the windows, one by the door from the hallway, and one near the hostages. Great. She should be grateful the pirates hadn't punished the hostages yet. Instead she wondered why.

"Is Hilario in there?"

He shook his head.

"The two of you hang back," said the younger sailor. "Don't come out unless we give the signal. We don't want you caught in the crossfire."

Brylie exchanged a look with Marcus. She'd wanted to hand over the responsibilities to someone else before, but now, allowing someone else to take charge made her shoulders tight. Huh. She'd been told she had control issues before. Clearly it was true.

The two men rolled into the room, measuring, then firing in controlled shots. One went wide, cracking the window behind one of the hostage takers. The next caught him high in the chest, the impact kicking him backwards, through the window. Beside her, Marcus choked out a swear, and then all was silent.

"Monica, are we clear?" Brylie called into the dining room, still hiding behind the door.

"What?" Monica's shrill voice answered.

"Are there any more?"

"No. No, that's it."

Still, none of them had been Hilario. Brylie hoped he was on the other ship and that Simon and his men were taking care of him. A moment passed before Brylie realized that Marcus had crossed to the fallen man by the door and was looking down at him, his brow creased in what looked like sorrow. Brylie watched him a moment before she was enveloped in Monica's arms. The other hostages rose as if awakening from a daze and wandered toward her.

"Is it over?"

Brylie heard gunfire from the other ship and hoped that it was. The two S.O.P. soldiers looked at each other, then motioned to Brylie they were going to help their comrades. They ducked through the shattered window and disappeared.

Suddenly Marcus whipped his gun up and aimed it into the center of the group. "You. Don't move."

Brylie twisted to see his target—the tall passenger that he called The Asshole.

"What are you doing?" the man demanded, raising his hands in surrender.

"You were working with them." He turned toward the two adventurers. "Tie him up."

The two young men moved slowly, still in shock, no doubt. Brylie jolted when a shot rang out from the open window. She saw a spark from the corner of her eye. Marcus swore and his gun clattered to the ground. She swept down to retrieve it.

"Leave it!" a heavily accented voice ordered when her hand hovered inches away.

She froze, then angled her head and looked up into the black, angry eyes of Hilario, who reached into the group and pulled the little blonde teenager, Trinity, in front of him, his arm hooked around her neck, his pistol aimed at her head. Her mother's keening cry echoed in the suddenly silent room.

"I am not leaving here empty handed. Drop the gun, little chef."

She glanced at Marcus, who shook his head, but Hilario pressed the gun tighter to Trinity's temple and the girl whimpered. Brylie crouched to place her weapon on the floor.

"Kick it over to Stephen."

Marcus made a sound of protest, and Brylie hesitated. To do that would give Hilario the upper hand again. But of course, she had the S.O.P. crew. Hilario had to know that. If she had some way of signaling Simon that they were in trouble again, that Hilario was here…

Stephen, the Asshole, stepped forward when she made no move to kick over the guns, and bent to retrieve them. Before she could move, Marcus kicked the man in the face, hard enough that she heard the crunch of bone. Blood splattered her jeans and she stepped back in horror. Marcus kicked him again, and Stephen grabbed his braced leg and pulled. Marcus went down on his back, hard, the air from his lungs escaping in a wheeze. Stephen flipped onto his stomach and grabbed at Marcus, who shifted out of the way as he fought to catch his breath. Stephen landed two punches on Marcus's face before rolling away and getting to his feet. Brylie screamed as the man spun, ready to kick Marcus in the ribs. Stephen's kick faltered and glanced off Marcus's hip.

Marcus used the momentum to flip onto his stomach. Then in a single movement, rocking back on his heels, he came up with a gun, which he leveled at Hilario's head.

"You can't shoot me without hurting the girl," Hilario taunted while Stephen groaned on the floor at her feet.

"Maybe not," Marcus said with a casual roll of his shoulders. He nodded toward the open window. "But he's got a pretty good bead on you."

Hilario pivoted, releasing Trinity enough that she could duck. Marcus fired at the same time Simon did from his position on the deck. Hilario spun, fell, and didn't move. Marcus turned back to Stephen, and gave him another kick before the two adventurers came to tie him up. Marcus let the gun fall to his side and drew his wounded hand against his waist.

It was over. Shaking, Brylie moved forward and grabbed his arm. "Are you okay? Joan!" Brylie called before he could respond.

He shook his head and rested his hand on his thigh, taking a few deep breaths. "She has enough to deal with, with the guys with hypothermia and these people in shock. I'll make sure Harris gives her a bonus for this cruise."

She caught the teasing note in his voice, and let herself lean into him, just for a moment, let him soothe her with his good hand stroking up and down her back. Looking anywhere but Hilario's body as Simon crouched over it.

Marcus drew her back, away from the body, away from the others who had come out of their shock and had begun milling around. "Let's go to my room. We can shower, get some sleep." The way his voice trailed off told her that wasn't all he wanted, and God, she wanted it too, wanted to lose herself in him, his touch, his kisses.

Reluctantly, she stepped back. "I need to get these people fed."

"So we put out some sandwich meat."

She shook her head. "No. they need a warm meal." And she needed to be back in her routine, to feel normal again. "Get some of the men to move tables into the lounge. I'll get my crew to work."

"Brylie." He curved his fingers on her cheek and forced her to look into his eyes. "You need sleep."

"I need this. Then I can sleep. Then we all can." She leaned into him for a moment. "It's over."

He stiffened at that and twisted to address Simon, who was securing Hilario, apparently still alive. "Find out who the other man who was helping them is. I heard them talking to someone else but didn't recognize his voice."

Simon nodded curtly, without looking up. Joan worked beside him to staunch the bleeding while Trinity's mother cradled the girl in her arms.

Then her father walked into the room. She pulled away from Marcus and crossed to him. He held out his arms and she buried her face in his broad chest, listening to his sound heartbeat as he folded his arms around her, lowered his head to hers with a short exhale of breath.

"My brave girl," he murmured.

"I've got to get to work," Brylie said, pulling free. "I'll feel better."

His expression was grim as he studied her face. He nodded and backed away, calling for help moving the tables as she motioned to her crew.

Being back in her kitchen was like being in an alien landscape after the hours—how many, she wondered—hiding and fighting back. Nearly an hour passed before she fell into the routine, deciding on a simple but tasty dish of mushroom chicken, mashed potatoes and salad. Simple, comforting food was what they needed after their ordeal. She wished Kayla, her pastry chef, was up to making a big, rich chocolate cake, but the poor girl was so shaken, Brylie sent her to her room.

She'd been working over an hour when she looked up to see Marcus standing against the wall, watching her.

"Is the lounge set up?" she asked, setting down the spatula.

He crossed to her and braced one hand on the counter. "And looking good. Most of the passengers returned to their cabins, but a few are in there, talking to Simon. He brought the other passengers back over, and he and the crew that is able will take Hilario's ship, with the prisoners, back to Hobart. He's taking our two guys with him."

"What, the passenger? Did they find out who the other crew member was?"

He shook his head. "No, I meant Jimmy and his friend. The—bodies."

"Oh. Good. I wondered."

"How are you holding up?" He stroked a bandaged hand down her arm.

She followed the movement, unable to meet his gaze, her emotions buried but ready to break free in a flood. Best to keep up the veneer for a bit longer. "I see you got that fixed up."

He lifted his hand in front of him. "For the time being. Trinity's mom is a nurse. She's helping Joan. I think she was a little rougher than she needed to be when she was wrapping it, probably because I put Trinity's life in danger."

"Everything worked out. I'm glad Joan has help." She moved away to toss the mushrooms simmering in butter. "You're hovering."

He grinned. "Put me to work."

She considered a moment. "Do you know how to bake a cake?"

CHAPTER EIGHT

Brylie was shaking with fatigue by the time the passengers were called back to the lounge, fed, and the kitchen cleaned and set up for the next meal. The passengers had devoured everything, including Marcus's cake, which was not pretty but very good. And now he stood waiting for her as she inspected her kitchen. He'd snagged her some of the cake, a plate of chicken and a bottle of wine because he was certain she hadn't eaten anything. Finally she nodded her approval and he tucked his arm through hers and guided her out of the kitchen.

He guided her to his room without protest, and tugged her sweatshirt over her head, shoved her jeans down her hips before turning her and prodding her toward the shower.

"The water should have warmed up by now. When I took mine, seemed everyone else had the same idea. I'll have to talk to Harris about that, too, more water heaters. Take as long as you like."

She did, letting the heat melt the knots in her muscles, washing away the stink of fear and adrenaline. She stood under the spray until it turned icy, then walking into Marcus's room wrapped in a thick robe to see her own fleece pajamas laid out on his bed. The familiarity, the comfort, his thoughtfulness—she gave a cry of delight and dropped the towel. She slipped into them quickly, mindless of her nakedness in front of him.

"You don't know how good it feels to be in my own clothes," she murmured, hugging herself.

"Come eat," he urged. "It's probably not as warm as it should be, but I know you didn't eat earlier."

"No." she crossed to the bed where he'd set up her dinner. "You're too good to me."

He snorted, and watched her eat. She finished her chicken, barely, and half a glass of wine before she could hardly keep her eyes open.

"Save me the cake for tomorrow. And wake me at six. In the morning," she murmured, reaching behind her to pull down the sheets. "I mean it, Marcus."

"You bet." He pulled away the table, tugged back the sheets so she could crawl in. By the time he took care of the food and settled into the bunk beside her, she was fast asleep.

***

He couldn't tell what woke him the next morning—the dip of the bunk, the brush of Brylie's hair against his cheek, or the whiff of minty breath. He opened his eyes to see her over him, her hair falling forward, the strands catching the rays of sun through the window. He barely had the chance to see her smile before she covered his mouth with hers.

He curved his hand over her hip and found bare skin. His lust surged, full-force, at the knowledge she was naked, and he trailed his touch up her back. She moaned her approval against his mouth and rolled her hips against his.

Hell, no. He wasn't going to be rushed, not after what they'd been through. He was going to savor every taste, every touch. He was going to make her come over and over, then she could fall asleep in his arms, and they'd wake up and do it again.

She seemed to have a different plan. Her hand pushed under his T-shirt, her fingers curling into his chest hair, playing with his nipple while her tongue slicked over his bottom lip. She broke the kiss to rub her lips over his stubbled jaw, then bit his earlobe. Beneath her hips, his erection jerked. Okay, well, maybe he'd let her set the pace this time. He got the feeling she wanted to be in control, and with his hand out of commission, he was fine with that.

She used her teeth again, just below his ear, and he went blind, just for a second.

"Jesus, Brylie."

"Help me get your shirt off. I want to feel you against me."

He blamed being barely awake on his awkwardness, his inability to anticipate her moves, his inability to make any of his own. Together they untangled his arms from the sweatshirt, then she was rubbing her breasts against his chest, her hand stroking down the line of hair and into his pants. Her hand closed around his sex at the same time she bit his nipple. Only years of experience kept him from coming right there.

He groaned her name, shoved her hand away with no small regret, and turned her to her side. Jesus, she was beautiful, the sunlight casting a pale glow on her porcelain skin, her lips parted on eager breaths, her nipples pale pink and hard, irresistible. Pushing her hair back with his injured hand, he mimicked her kisses—lips, jaw, ear, drawing out the one beneath her ear until she squirmed, hooking her leg over his thighs. All he had to do was shift his hips forward and he'd be inside her.

"Not yet." He had to taste her nipples, had to feel her reaction to him suckling her. He sipped the stiff little peak between his lips and she arched against him, grabbing his good hand in both of hers and urging it down her belly. She whispered his name again and again, her voice tight with need, but he resisted the pull. Instead, he savored the pliant flesh beneath his tongue, rolled it, sucked it, bit down lightly. Her cry was hoarse, and he looked up to make sure he hadn't hurt her. But no, her lips were parted in pleasure, her eyelids were heavy with it. He dropped a soft kiss to the tender skin, then continued to trail kisses down over her flat belly, blowing a breath over the strawberry curls at the juncture of her thighs. She parted them and he moved lower, hooking her knees over his shoulders. Her breathing was ragged now in anticipation. He grinned, and bent to taste her.

She came hard, on a keening cry, at the first touch of his mouth. He wanted to stay, to take her pleasure higher, but she reached for him, pulling him up her body.

"I want you inside me," she said, before closing her mouth over his.

Christ, that was sexy. He might have resisted, only he wanted the same thing, to drive into her, feel her body clasp around him. He reached for the nightstand but she wiggled a packet in front of him.

"God, Marcus, hurry."

She sheathed him and turned him onto his back, rising over him, and then he was inside her. His moan mingled with hers as she gripped him, her body slick and warm. She took him deeper with a shift of hips. He drew her down and covered her mouth with his, stroking her pretty legs, her pretty hair, smelling her scent all around him. Perfect, perfect. He felt her desire rising, felt it in her breathing, her pulse, the slickness of her body around him. God, she was beautiful as she straightened over him, reaching for her orgasm, bringing him to the brink of his.

He reached over and yanked up the shade so the sunlight shone on her creamy skin, then arched his hips to press into her. She shuddered around him, over him, her body undulating with her orgasm. The sight of her, head tossed back, mouth open on a cry of pleasure, the feeling of her squeezing him, dragged him over the edge with a shout.

She draped herself over him, her breathing ragged, her hair brushing his lips, her body limp. He pulled her hair away from her face and pressed a kiss to her forehead, wanting nothing more than to savor her for as long as it took to get back to port. He wasn't sure if she'd go for it, but he'd been known to be pretty persuasive.

Before he could ease her onto the bed, someone pounded on the door. She jolted and rolled from the bunk, grabbing the blanket from the end of the bed to cover herself. Marcus discarded the condom in the wastebasket, reached for his sweats, and stepped toward the door.

"Who is it?"

"Captain Winston. We need to talk."

Oh, hell. Marcus swung his gaze toward Brylie, whose eyes had gone wide. He hadn't had to worry about being caught by a girl's daddy since he was a teenager. Brylie scrambled for her sweatshirt, and tugged it on.

"Just give me a second," Marcus called.

"It's important."

"Yeah, just a minute." He couldn't get Brylie out of here without her father seeing. "Go to the bathroom."

She shook her head and swung her bare legs over the edge of the bunk. She drew on her pajama bottoms and nodded for Marcus to open the door. He frowned, giving her a moment to reconsider. Instead, she moved past him and turned the handle, admitting her father.

"What is it, Captain?" Marcus asked brightly.

The man glanced over his shoulder and no doubt saw Brylie, because he drew in his chin and his face reddened. Marcus jolted when she placed her hand on his arm. His own face heated, but he forced himself to meet the older man's thunderous gaze. Oh, hell.

"Can I come in? This isn't something I want to discuss in the hall."

Come in. Where the only place to sit was on the bed where Marcus had just made love to his daughter. "Um. Sure." He stepped back, and from the corner of his eye saw that Brylie had tugged the bedspread over the mattress. Marcus bent to scoop his sweatshirt from the floor. Not that the old man could have a doubt about what had just gone on here. Until now, Marcus hadn't noticed the marks his stubble had made on Brylie's pale skin, the effect of his hands in her hair.

But the captain didn't say anything, barely glanced at his daughter. "The plane carrying the ransom left Australia before the attack on the patrol ship. It fell out of radio contact a few hours ago, and began emitting an emergency beacon within the past hour, from the continent."

"The continent? Antarctica?" Brylie asked.

He nodded, rubbing his big hands together, rocking on his feet as if anxious to escape the tiny compartment. Marcus kept an eye on those big hands, waiting to see one flying at his face any minute now.

"The plane is on Antarctica?" Marcus forced himself to ask. "Will they send the patrol to them?"

"They will. But we're closer. And…your brother Harris was on the plane, accompanying the ransom money."

Marcus froze in the act of pulling on his sweatshirt and his blood chilled. "Harris was on the plane?"

The captain nodded. "I'm sorry, son."

His chest squeezed so hard he could barely get the words out. "And there's been no radio contact?"

"I'm afraid not."

His mind spun. Harris, on the continent, in the cold. "How far away are we?"

"Three hours."

Marcus scrubbed his hand over his face. "How can that be? We've been heading north all night."

"Northwest, not far from the continent."

"So we can go find them."

"No, not we," Brylie protested. "You don't know the continent, the weather, the terrain. There are trained people who can do this."

He pivoted on her. "My brother is out there. He came because I'm here. I can't just leave him out there. I know cold weather—I'm a snowboarder, damn it. I'm going to find my brother." He turned back to her father. "How do we get to Antarctica?"

***

Brylie packed the survival pack with power bars, packets of cereal, chocolate bars and biscuits. She'd done this before for tourists who wanted to see Antarctica in person, like Jimmy's friends out there. Only now she was sending her lover there, looking for his brother. Jimmy's friends had agreed—reluctantly after Marcus refused to allow them to accompany them to the peninsula—to let Marcus wear Jimmy's gear since he hadn't packed anything appropriate. Carl would be taking him on the sightseeing helicopter. Brylie had protested—the helicopter wasn't equipped to bring back injured people. Her father had silenced her with a look that told her he doubted there would be survivors. But Marcus was the boss, and he was frantic to see his brother.

He walked into the kitchen then, moving differently with his layers of clothing, with a kind of confidence she hadn't seen in him. He'd been confident in the bar in Hobart, but his attitude then had been different, almost arrogant. But this—this was new. This was—sexy as hell.

The wrong thing to be thinking as he went off to find his missing brother. He crossed to her, not meeting her gaze, which made her uneasy. He checked the pack and nodded approvingly.

She bit the inside of her lip. Acting on impulse never worked well for her, but, "I want to go with you," she blurted.

His gaze shot to hers, his eyes flat, unreadable. "No."

"I wasn't asking." She zipped up the pack and slid it toward him on the counter.

He pressed his lips together, and gave her a cursory inspection. "You don't have the right clothes."

She snapped her heels together and squared her shoulders. "I do, at least warm enough for the flight over the peninsula to the crash site." The beacon that transmitted told them the site was on the west side of the peninsula, near the mountain range.

He shook his head and turned his attention back to the pack, though she'd secured it. "You're safer here."

"I don't give a shit about being safe." She braced her hands on the counter and glared. But she couldn't say what she wanted to say, that she wanted to be there with him, be there for him, as he looked for his brother.

He stepped forward and curved his hand over her cheek. "You've been through enough the past few days."

"You've been through exactly the same thing."

"My brother is out there." He took a step back and scrubbed a hand over his hair. "Christ, Brylie. I don't want to chance it. While the weather is supposed to be good, it's too risky."

"It's dangerous for you, too."

"I can take care of myself."

She drew back, catching his meaning. He didn't want to take care of anyone else. Right. "I can too. Believe that

I've been doing it a long time." She pushed the pack toward him. "I'll meet you at the helicopter."

***

Marcus's stomach gripped when Brylie crossed the small landing pad, toward the helicopter where he and Carl had loaded the gear they'd need—the food and water Brylie had gathered, blankets and sleeping bags, and a first aid kit Joan had packed. Brylie moved stiffly, which let him know she was well-insulated in layers. Which meant she'd be just fine if he locked her in the freezer while he took off.

He'd never known anyone so damned stubborn.

Except, well, him.

She looked dressed warm enough in a sweater that covered her chin and wrists, heavy shoes, a warm coat, a knit cap, and gloves that would give her hands flexibility. Even in the summer, frostbite was a real danger, with temperatures that could get down to single digits Celsius, though the weather on the peninsula was the mildest in Antarctica, thanks to the proximity to the ocean.

The smile she gave him was forced as she stopped a few feet away. "I'm ready."

He could have argued harder. Hell, he could have convinced her father to step in and stop her. But the truth was, part of him was glad she'd be with him. He knew how to work with her, knew he could count on her. He was sure Carl was fine, too, but he trusted Brylie.

When he didn't say anything, she squared her shoulders. "You'll be glad I'm there. I'll make myself useful."

She didn't sound like she believed it herself. He had to wonder what her motivation was. Okay, he had an idea, and that scared him almost as much as what he'd find when he got to the airplane. Almost as scary as his reason for wanting her to come along.

"Come on, then." Carl climbed into the pilot's seat and motioned them into the six-seater.

Marcus looked into the back—room for a stretcher if need arose. But only one. How many had been on the plane when it went down? Good thing he had told Evan and Michael they couldn't come along.

Yeah, he knew what he might find. How many people survived plane crashes, after all? But he couldn't take the chance that his brother could be alive and needing help while Marcus sat on his ass and waited for someone else to take over. Hadn't he done that plenty of times in the past? Time to grow up.

His stomach dipped as the rotors started and the helicopter lifted away from the deck, Carl's hand steady on the control. He rose above the ship, and the passengers who'd come out to watch their departure, then dipped and headed toward the peninsula.

Once Marcus caught his breath, he leaned toward the passenger window to look at the scenery below, the unbelievably blue water crashing on the black rocks of the shore, the icebergs dotting the ocean, the endless stretch of white ahead of them. They were approaching from the tip of the peninsula and flying down the west side of the mountain range, following the beacon on the GPS Marcus carried. The three of them had GPS trackers on their clothing as well, just in case.

Brylie touched his arm. He twisted to look at her, and she pointed out the window ahead of them. He turned to see several dots on the edge of the white terrain, close to the beach. Without being told, Carl took the helicopter lower. Marcus leaned forward to see the dots were seals on the beach—hundreds of them, some of them lying on the shore, some moving in and out of the water. Brylie reached past him to point at the water, where he could see them swimming below the surface, fast as lightning, so at odds with their lumbering movements on land. He turned to grin at Brylie, something he hadn't thought he'd be able to do after hearing about the plane crash. She grinned in return, then settled back to watch the seals until they were out of sight.

"Where are the penguins?" he asked over the noise of the rotor.

"Should be along any minute. You want to go sightseeing or look for your brother?" Carl demanded, taking the helicopter higher.

"Right." He checked the GPS signal. It didn't seem to be any closer, though they were traveling pretty damned fast.

The wind bumped the helicopter beneath them, taking them up a few feet, then dropping them, no more than a roller coaster would do, and he laughed off the nervousness. Yeah, he'd been some pretty high places, but he'd been in control—or mostly in control.

He forced himself to stop watching the blip on the screen. The scenery below was really amazing, mountains to the left of him so steep they didn't even tempt him to snowboard down them.

"They're thought to be part of the Andes mountain chain." Brylie pitched her voice to be heard. "Scientists think that without the ice cap, these would be a series of islands instead."

She was trying to distract him from what he'd find, he knew, and appreciated it, but all he could show her was a nod.

She edged forward and pointed to the water again. "This will probably be our last trip this summer. The sea ice is already reforming. We can usually get in another cruise, but it looks like fall is coming early this year."

"How many times have you been to the continent?" he asked.

"A few dozen. Never more than a couple of hours. I have gotten up close with a penguin or two. I like the gentoo ones. Very funny."

They continued in silence. As the blip got closer, Marcus wanted nothing more than to hold Brylie's hand. As he looked at the landscape, he couldn't see this ending well. Enough of the plane was intact if the beacon was still going off, but that said nothing about the passengers. How long had they been out here now? Seven hours? He checked the outside temperature on Carl's controls. Four degrees Celsius. Survivable. Miserable, but survivable.

The blip grew closer and Marcus strained to look out the window, trying to find the crash site visually. Would it be in one piece or several? The blowing snow on the surface made everything hard to see. For all he knew, it could have covered up the plane already.

No, there it was, broken in two, missing a wing. His pulse skipped—hope or fear, he couldn't name. Carl pointed to what looked like an engine several hundred feet away. The plane had crashed before it reached the mountain. At least Harris had a chance of surviving.

He checked on Brylie again. "You have the space blankets ready?"

She patted the pocket of the survival bag she'd packed.

Just then, the helicopter dipped again, and this time Carl cursed, muttering about goddamned wind shears. Above them, the sound of the rotor changed from a chug to a whine, and instead of ascending after they did after the last bump, they continued on a downward incline. For a moment, Marcus hoped Carl was taking them in close to look at penguins or something, but the flow of obscenities from the man's mouth made that doubtful. The older man's arms flexed with the effort to pull the helicopter up, to no avail. Above them, the rotors slowed. Dread clumped in Marcus's throat.

"What the hell?"

Carl shook his head. "Not now."

"Can I help?"

Just then the rotors stopped, and everything was deathly quiet. Then the helicopter tipped its nose down and plummeted to the earth.

CHAPTER NINE

Marcus's back hurt like hell, and he was goddamned cold. He opened his eyes and saw nothing but white in front of him. He squeezed his eyes shut and opened them again. Right. Snow. It had poured in through the broken windshield and coated the console, where it was splashed with red.

He whipped his head—bad idea—to see Carl slumped away from him, a gash slicing from his temple to mid-cheek, deep. Marcus watched for the rise and fall of the other man's chest, but didn't see it.

Brylie.

He pivoted toward the backseat, nearly strangling himself with the seatbelt. She was out, her head lolled to one side, but no blood, and he could see she was breathing.

Thank God.

He fumbled to release his seatbelt and lunged toward her. "Brylie." He worked her seatbelt free and she went limp against him. "Oh, hell, no." He reached beneath her jaw to feel her pulse. There, and strong, and now she stirred in his arms. Those reddish-blonde eyelashes fluttered and she looked up at him.

"Marcus?"

"The helicopter went down. Are you hurt?"

She frowned and shifted on the seat as if testing herself out. "Everywhere. But no place in particular. You?"

He wasn't thinking about that now. "Help me with Carl."

"How long have we been down?" she asked as he climbed between the seats to check out Carl.

Shit, his right ankle was messed up. Sprained or broken, he couldn't tell yet, and wouldn't try to figure it out until they helped Carl.

"No idea."

Though come to think of it, he wasn't too cold, considering the windshield was broken, so it couldn't have been long. He unbuckled the seatbelt as Brylie opened the first aid kit he wasn't sure they'd need. He checked the older man's pulse as he'd done Brylie's. Nothing. Shit. He trailed his hands down Carl's arm. Nothing. His chest—no. But his body was still warm.

"Help me get him into the back seat." If he could stretch him out, he and Brylie could perform CPR. Marcus had learned when he'd become a snowboarder, though he hadn't been recertified in a while.

Together he and Brylie wrested the older man into something of a prone position, a trick with Marcus's bad hand.

"Chest or mouth?" he asked.

Since she was wedged in a position near his head, she made a face, her gaze on the blood coating one side of his face. "Mouth."

"Right." He opened Carl's coat for better contact. "You know how to do this?"

"You count."

Keeping his good arm straight, he pumped Carl's chest, then watched as Brylie formed a seal around his mouth and blew. She rose up as Marcus pumped again, keeping her hand braced against the back of the pilot's seat before she bent to blow again. They made a good team, aware of each other, so he soon was able to stop counting.

And then Carl sucked in a deep breath. Brylie rolled back on her heels to rest against the side of the helicopter as the old man blinked, trying to get his bearings. Marcus zipped up Carl's coat again. He'd worked up a sweat, but the old guy might be cold.

Carl rolled onto his elbow and tried to push himself up. Marcus stopped him with a hand to his chest.

"Take it easy. You have a pretty good gash there." He pointed to his own head.

Carl lifted his hand to his head and pulled it away to look at the blood. "We crashed?"

"Looks like."

"Where?"

"I don't think we're far from where the plane went down." Marcus leaned back into the front seat and searched for the GPS tracker. He swore when a piece of metal sticking up through the floor sliced through his glove and into his finger. Suddenly exhausted, he leaned heavily against the side of his seat.

Brylie shifted onto her knees and touched his cheek. "Are you hurt?"

"I'm all right. Just need to find that doohickey."

She grabbed his bleeding hand and drew off his glove. His finger was bleeding pretty good. "What happened here?"

"Floorboard's torn up pretty bad. Maybe the tracker fell out."

She scowled at the injury. "Hope you're up to date on your tetanus. You may need stitches."

"Won't be the first time. I had a shot a couple years back. Can't remember just what that injury was, though."

"Put pressure on it," she told him, reaching back for the first aid kit.

He let her disinfect it, but drew a line at stitches. "Just wrap it for now." His leg muscles were quivering from being cramped between the seats, and while he was worried about their situation, he was also thinking of his brother, and how he would get to him now. How far from the plane had they crashed?

"Might be a good idea to get out of here," Carl echoed his thoughts, using the back of the seat to pull himself up to a sitting position. "No telling how stable we are."

"I'll go see. See if I can find the tracker, too."

Marcus needed to get out of here anyway, feeling too confined, needing to know what situation they were in. He tugged his torn glove back on and shoved at the door, but it was jammed. Of course. He climbed across to the pilot's seat and found that door even worse. Great. He dropped into his seat and, lifting his legs above the console, he kicked out what remained of the windshield. Safety glass showered down on him.

"Okay back there?" he asked over his shoulder, and saw that Brylie had covered Carl's face with one of the space blankets. Good thinking.

"Don't go far," she said, her voice tight.

He met her gaze. "Don't worry. I'm just going to walk around the helicopter, and maybe see if I can see the plane from where we are. I'll be back in a minute."

When he climbed out, he understood her concern. Snow was blowing everywhere. He could easily get turned around and lost in this, especially if the snow covered his tracks and drifted against the helicopter.

The blowing snow probably meant that the damned tracker was buried, too. Great.

The good news was, the helicopter was on solid ground, no chance of it tumbling off a cliff or into a crevasse. He marched up the shifting snow to stand as close to the battered rotor as he could, and looked out over the landscape. Yeah, hell of a lot easier to see from above. All he saw now was white, everywhere. He couldn't even see the mountains. And since the sun was on the other side of the mountains, everything here was in shadow.

"Marcus!" Brylie's voice called from under his feet.

He slid down the slope, keeping his feet under him— he didn't want to get wet if he didn't have to—and walked back to the broken window. Brylie was leaning on his seat, holding the tracker in her gloved hand. And they were right on top of the beeping.

***

Already Brylie was cold beneath her thermal underclothes, her knit shirt, flannel shirt, sweater and coat, her two pairs of socks and flannel-lined jeans. The wind was dry, and while it was behind them, it still managed to work its way through the layers.

The snow felt weird underfoot, shifty, more like sand than precipitation. The inside of her nose was dry from the lack of humidity in the air. But she wouldn't say anything, since she had asked to come along.

She kept a concerned eye on Carl, who staggered, and Marcus, who limped, though he hadn't said anything about injuring his leg. The idea was to get to the plane, since it looked like most of the fuselage was intact, and hole up there until the rescue plane came. That way they'd know what happened to Harris and the crew, could help them if they were able, and would have more room. She didn't know if it would be warmer, but she would prefer it to being trapped in the tiny helicopter.

"We'll have to make sure it's secure before we go in," Carl said. "Don't want to be inside if it decides to slide down a slope."

Marcus nodded, but Brylie noticed his shoulders were tight. Pain or fear? She powered forward to catch up with him. She wished she could see his eyes beneath the polarized lenses.

"Are you hurt?" she asked.

"Crash screwed up my right leg a bit."

"Cut?"

He shook his head.

"Marcus."

"I'll be fine once I know how my brother is."

She opened her mouth and he held up his hand.

"I'm going to do this."

"And you're not going to tell me if you can't?"

"Brylie. I've boarded down mountains in worse shape." He curled his hand around hers and matched his stride to hers as they made their way toward the remains of the plane.

The closer they got, the more hopeful she felt. The fuselage was in two parts and had lost a wing and an engine, but the front part of the plane didn't seem to have a lot of damage. The open part of the fuselage was angled toward the mountain, so maybe the inside wasn't as cold as it might have been. Marcus broke away from her and lunged forward, shouting Harris's name. As he got closer, he slapped his hand on the outside of the plane. Only because she was watching, Brylie saw him hesitate when he reached the ragged opening. She tried to catch up, but couldn't reach him before he disappeared into the plane. His shout sent chills through her body. She slipped, dropping to her knees hard enough to drive her breath from her body before she scrambled upright and into the plane after him.

She passed Carl and skidded around the shredded skin of the aircraft, and stepped inside. The plane listed about thirty degrees against the side of the mountain, so all the chairs were at an angle and detritus littered the ground beneath her, where the wall met the floor. She peered into the plane, letting her eyes adjust to the dim light. No sign of Marcus. As she moved deeper into the plane, she heard him, muttering and swearing. She followed the sound, her stomach tight with fear of what she'd see.

She passed one of the seats to see a man slumped against the wall between the fuselage and the cockpit, Marcus crouched over him, muttering. The man wasn't dressed for the weather—wearing only a thin white shirt, now coated with blood, and slacks. His lips were blue.

"Marcus?"

"He's alive. Hurt bad, but alive. Give me a—"

He held out his hand and she put a space blanket into it. He flashed her a grateful smile and tucked it around the man who must be his brother.

"The others?" she asked.

He cast a guilty glance toward the cockpit. "I haven't checked. I'll—"

"I'll do it." She didn't want to see, but he clearly wanted—needed—to be with his brother. With a shaking hand, she reached for the latch to the cockpit door. It was jammed, so she had to pull, and she jumped back with a scream when a body tumbled out at her feet.

Marcus half-rose, half-turned toward her. "Christ. Is he dead?"

He couldn't be otherwise, not with all that blood. She took in a deep breath—bad idea, because now her mouth was filled with a coppery taste—and bent to touch the man's chest. No movement, and his body was cold and stiff. Through slitted eyes, she saw a gouge in the side of his throat, no doubt the source of the blood that covered his white shirt.

"Anyone else?" Marcus asked, his voice strangled.

Finding out meant stepping over the pilot's body. She swallowed the bile rising in her throat and stretched her leg out, finding footing between the dead man's legs and using the door frame to pull herself into the cockpit. A groan from the seat to her right made her jump. She stumbled when her foot came down on the dead man's thigh. A strong hand behind her steadied her.

"He's alive," she told Carl and righted herself. "Let me see."

"Why are these guys unbuckled?" Marcus demanded from the other side of the wall. "Didn't they know the plane was going down?"

"Maybe they unbuckled after they landed," Carl said. "There's smeared blood on the straps there."

She edged into the tiny cockpit and touched the co-pilot's shoulder. "Hey, are you conscious? Where are you hurt?" Blood was everywhere but she couldn't see the source. His right sleeve was soaked. He, too, was cold, not dressed for the weather. "Carl, I need a blanket."

"Shoulder," the man murmured. "Side. Thigh."

"Can you get out of the seat? I'll help you."

He rolled brown eyes up at her. "If I could, I would have, don't you think?"

She rocked on her heels and pushed her hood back, considering. The cockpit was very small, not much room to maneuver, even without the body. She was going to have to move the body—Marcus and Carl were too injured.

"Are there only the three of you?"

"Is Drew dead?"

"The pilot? Yes. I'm sorry."

The man blew out a breath. "I figured. Yes, only the three of us, then."

"What's your name?" She reached around to unbuckle his seatbelt. "I'm Brylie."

"I'm George. Where did you come from?"

"We're from the ship. We heard about the crash—Marcus had to see about his brother." She thought it probably wasn't a good idea to tell him they'd crashed as well, not yet. "I'm going to move Drew, and then I'll help you." She wanted to ask what had happened, but that could wait until she'd stopped his bleeding. She moved gingerly around Drew's prone body, back into the main body of the plane and straightened, her hands on her hips. Drew was a big guy. She considered, then bent and looped her hands under his arms.

"What are you doing?" Marcus's voice was sharp behind her.

She tugged and grunted. "I need to move him out of the way. I can't get to the co-pilot."

He edged her aside and grasped the pilot's arm to pull him into the body of the plane. "Here."

Together, they maneuvered Drew through the door and down the hall. "How is Harris?"

Marcus's mouth thinned. "It's bad. We better hope that the rescue comes soon."

"Rescue?" George leaned into the doorway to look at them. "I thought you were the rescue."

"Yeah, well, that was the plan." Marcus nudged Brylie behind a seat and took her place, pulling the big man down the aisle into the snow outside the fuselage.

"Marcus," she protested, looking past him into the snow.

He straightened. "I'm sorry for it, but there's no room."

She moved toward the cockpit and ducked so George could loop his arm around her shoulders. When she straightened, she felt the strain through her already battered body. She guided him from his seat, through the narrow door, and carefully helped him stretch out on the floor, his feet to Harris's. She retrieved the blanket that had dragged free and covered his legs while she unbuttoned his shirt to examine his wound.

Carl sat on the seat behind her and leaned over her shoulder. He sucked in a breath when she exposed the gash in the co-pilot's side.

"That's going to take more than a bandage."

No kidding. She wasn't equipped to deal with this. She avoided George's questioning gaze as she inspected the wound, so he lifted his head to try to see. She pushed his head back to the floor.

"I'll—take care of it." Though she had no idea how.

***

Marcus slumped against the wall of the fuselage beside Brylie and rested his arms on his knees. Both their patients were as stable as they could make them after Brylie applied pressure bandages to George and Marcus warmed his brother the best he could. A concussion was most likely, but there was nothing they could do about it. Carl snored along the wall against the cockpit. She worried about him sleeping in the cold, but reasoned their location in the front of the plane was warm enough, with the lantern and body heat. Brylie had scavenged the plane, and in addition to the paraffin lantern they'd brought from the wrecked helicopter, she'd found pillows and blankets. She'd hung one of the blankets over the opening of the plane. While it didn't cover the entire opening, it did cut some of the wind. Carl huddled beneath another, along with a space blanket. She was so cold she could barely move her hands, though she'd put her gloves back on after patching up George's wounds and curled up with Marcus in a nest of blankets against the bulkhead.

"Are you going to let me look at your leg now?"

"Nothing you can do." He pulled an energy bar out of the pack and offered her one. She shook her head, but he held it out insistently. "You need to eat. Your body needs more calories in the cold."

She took it reluctantly. "Has Harris regained consciousness?"

He shook his head. "I don't know how long I can keep him going."

"The rescue plane should be here in a couple of hours." She had no idea how long—a flight from Australia to Antarctica was usually about four hours, but who knew, with the weather, and preparations they'd have to make beforehand. Maybe two, maybe three, maybe longer. "Is your ankle broken?"

He shifted his gaze without moving his head. "Hairline fracture, probably. I've had worse."

"Let me see it."

"Nothing you can do," he repeated, but shoved up his pants anyway.

The skin above his boot was swollen and almost purple. She couldn't help the gasp of alarm. "We need to get the boot off."

He shook his head. "Won't be able to get it back on, and who knows if we'll have to walk out of this place. Don't want frostbite."

"At least unlace it." God. Her stomach roiled and she skimmed her hand over the swollen skin. It was hot to the touch. "You've been walking on that?"

He drew in a sharp breath. "Not if I can help it."

"Should we wrap it up to give it some kind of support?"

He pulled his pants back into place. "Let's just wait. You said they won't be long."

She hoped.

"You're shivering." He shifted and pulled a blanket over both of them. "Come here." He wrapped his arm around her, unzipped his jacket and pulled her against his side.

His body heat penetrated through his layers of clothes. She curled her fist into the front of his shirt. She wanted so badly to fall asleep listening to the beat of his heart, but in this cold, she knew that would be a mistake. So she sought for a topic of conversation. Her gaze fell on his brother, taking in his lined face and graying brown hair, a shade lighter than Marcus's.

"How much older is Harris than you?"

"Eight years."

"Are you close?"

He snorted a laugh. "Not at all. Do you have any brothers or sisters?"

She shifted to look up at him, not letting him turn the conversation around on her. "If you're not close, why did he come out here with the ransom?"

He shrugged. "Guilt, maybe? He sent me on this trip, figured he had to bail me out, again."

"Which is why you aren't close."

"You didn't answer my question. Brothers and sisters?"

She huffed out a breath. She didn't want to talk about herself, but at least the conversation was taking his mind off their predicament. "Only child."

"Must have been rough when your parents split, being on your own. How old were you?"

"Twelve. I didn't mind too much." She twisted her hands in the hem of her sweatshirt. "I like being by myself."

He chuckled. "Which is why you work in a hot room full of frantic people on a cruise ship?"

She smiled. "Probably why I like being by myself so much."

"Tell me what happened to chase you out of New York."

She really didn't want to talk about that, let him know what an idiot she'd been. Shame burned her cheeks. She hadn't let Marcus see too many of her weaknesses, and those he'd seen were based on emotion, not poor choices. "I don't want to talk about it." In fact she hadn't, to anyone. Not even her father knew the reason she'd fled to Australia to work on his cruise ship.

"You think I've never made a mistake? How do you think I ended up on the Ice Queen?" He flexed his good hand to remind her of the fight that sent him here. "So 'fess up."

She sighed. Why not tell him? They didn't have the possibility of a future anyway. He was the boss and, well, she didn't know if she could go back on that ship again after this cruise anyway. "A guy. It's always a guy. Ethan said he was divorced. His wife Lily thought otherwise. She was very powerful, had a lot of friends and a lot of money, and she burned me. I couldn't get another job in the state, and then when I went to San Francisco, she found out and burned me there, too."

He blew out a whistle. "Pretty harsh, seeing as her husband was to blame."

She tucked her hair behind her ear. "Yeah, well, I probably shouldn't have been so eager to believe him."

"You were a kid."

She shifted to look up at him. "What makes you say that?"

"Because you're not that old now."

She wanted to take the out he offered her, but couldn't offer up an excuse for her behavior. "You know as well as I do that being a kid isn't an excuse. I was perfectly willing to act as a grown-up with him." She didn't want to discuss her former sex life with Marcus, didn't want him thinking about her with another man. Didn't want to think about Ethan when she was with Marcus, how slimy she'd felt, inside and out, when she learned he was still married.

Marcus's tone was anything but lascivious when he asked, "How long were you together?"

"Four months." Four exciting months when she'd been the toast of the town and madly in love. Rising up so high had only made her fall hurt that much more.

He sucked in a breath through his teeth. "Big price to pay for a short time."

No kidding. The bruises to her pride—and her heart—were still tender. "My decision."

"Would you go back to New York if you could?"

Trick question. Did he want to know as her lover, so he'd know how far apart they'd be once this was over? Or as her employer, who'd have to find another chef if she went back? Or was he just curious? She took a deep breath and gave him the honest answer.

"I loved New York. There was energy there, and I was good at what I did, Marcus. You haven't really seen that, but I'm good at what I do. One little mistake put me in exile."

He rested his head against the side of the fuselage with a sigh. Of course he'd know what that was like. Wasn't he here for the same reason?

"Think we've learned our lesson?" he asked.

"It's easier for you to go back than me."

"Nah, I won't snowboard again. And I'm pretty sure I don't want to be a medic, not after today." He nodded toward Harris's prone form.

Time to divert his attention again. "So why are you a snowboarder? I wouldn't think there's that much snow in Australia."

"New Zealand, though." His grin colored his voice. "My family enjoyed ski vacations. And I was too stubborn to enjoy what my family did, so I found other outlets. The snowboarders I met were cool—tattooed and pierced, and they made my parents nervous, so of course I was drawn to them."

"But you don't have any tattoos or piercings."

He chuckled and tapped his earlobe, then his lower lip. "My piercings closed up, and I never could decide what I wanted for a tattoo. Decisions aren't exactly my thing. For example, a career. I came out on the Ice Queen thinking I'd find it. Needing to find it. Now, shit. I don't know."

"What about running security on the ships? I think you'd be good at it, especially now that you see where the gaps are. It might be hard at first, but you're a good problem solver."

He jolted, then shifted to look down at her. "I'm a what? What makes you say that?"

She lifted a shoulder. "You thought fast, you worked through until you found solutions, and you weren't afraid to act on them."

He settled back against the side of the plane and didn't speak for a bit. "I'm not scared of hard work. I just don't really like being shot at and crashing."

His indignant tone surprised a laugh out of her. He grinned in return and curved his gloved fingers under her chin, lifting her face for his kiss.

His mouth was warm and tasted of the fruit bar he'd just eaten, sweet, with a hint of spice. She curled into him, drawing a hiss of pain when she accidentally bumped his leg.

"Sorry! Sorry," she murmured, but he pulled her back in for another kiss, reaching for her hips to lift her over him, to straddle him. "Very important things can freeze off," she warned.

"I'm not getting naked, just using body heat." He unzipped her coat and wrapped his arms around her waist beneath the bulk of it, then skimmed his hand over her breast, and her shiver had nothing to do with the cold.

This was such a bad idea, rubbing up against him, considering who he was, especially when she didn't know what the future would hold. She hadn't let herself think about that when they'd been hiding from the terrorists, and didn't want to think about it now. His kisses were incredible—and apparently she'd learned nothing from her New York experience. Not that she thought Marcus would set her off the ship when he was tired of her—no, he'd be the one to walk away.

Like that would hurt any less.

So she should be the one to pull away. She just didn't have the strength to do it yet.

He broke the kiss and nuzzled her throat, dragging her hips forward, snug against his and the rising erection she felt through the layer of clothes. She slipped her fingers under the knit of his hat to stroke his hair, savoring everything, knowing soon she'd no longer have it.

A groan from the front of the plane drew their attention. In a flash, he broke the kiss and set her aside, climbing to his knees. He'd clearly forgotten about his leg, because he winced when the toe of his boot touched the floor.

"I'll go." She put her hand on his arm to stop him.

"It's my brother." He tossed the blankets tangling about him aside and edged past George to reach Harris.

Brylie followed, gripping the back of the chair as Marcus crouched and touched Harris's face. Harris turned his head toward Marcus.

"Where am I?"

"Antarctica. I'd ask you why if you hadn't been unconscious for the past few hours."

Harris slitted his eyes against the dim light. "I thought you were on the ship. I thought you needed to be ransomed."

"Got myself out of the scrape this time, just to see if you'd notice. Hey, take it easy," he said when Harris tried to turn, and he pressed a hand to his brother's shoulder to keep him still. "We don't know how bad you're hurt."

"What happened?"

"Your plane crashed. I came to save you for a change."

Harris curled up in an attempt to sit, but Marcus kept his grip firm. "So what are we waiting for? I'm so cold my balls—" He glanced past Marcus and saw Brylie, stopping the flow of words. "Let's get out of here."

"Slight problem with the plan." Marcus told him quickly about how the helicopter crashed and they were awaiting rescue themselves.

"Nice plan." Harris rested his head on the pillow Marcus had tucked behind him. "How long will that be?"

"We're out of radio contact right now. I can't say. Do you remember what happened before you crashed?"

Harris tried to shake his head, but stopped abruptly, eyes narrowed in pain.

"Why weren't you buckled in?" Marcus asked.

Harris scowled. "I was."

"Not when we got here."

"Who's we?" Harris's gaze turned back to Brylie. "Are you Brylie?"

"I am."

"My brother got you into more trouble?"

"Looks like."

"You have to watch out for him. That's his specialty. How did you get away from the pirates?"

He listened as they told him about the rescue ship and their need to fight back on their own. His eyes drifted shut as if keeping them open took too much energy. "You're lucky you didn't get killed. That no one on board got killed because of your decision."

Marcus gritted his teeth. "Yeah, thanks for that."

"Could have been a big lawsuit. Bad enough we still have fall-out from the thing with the senator's son."

Brylie saw the flash of pain on Marcus's face that had nothing to do with his injuries. Then his expression changed to something she hadn't seen since she first spotted him in the bar in Hobart. It was almost a sneer that broadcast an I-don't-give-a-shit attitude. She winced, recognizing it for the mask it was, and she wanted to reach out to him, to ground him, but he was already pushing to his feet.

"That you remember, but you don't know how you crashed." Marcus turned and hobbled past Brylie to the back of the plane.

Brylie watched him go, her heart urging her to go after him, her mind reminding her that they were too much alike, that he needed to nurse his pain in private. Instead, she took Marcus's place at Harris's side.

"You're too hard on him," she chided, tucking the blanket more securely about Harris's shoulders. Odd she should feel so comfortable confronting him after only a few conversations with him on the sat phone. After all, he was more her boss than Marcus. But her need to defend Marcus defeated her usual sense of self-preservation. "He came out here because he was worried about you."

"He came out here because he's impulsive. Reckless. You should know that."

She drew back as if he'd slapped her. "You don't know me."

He softened his tone. "You're right. I don't. I'm sorry. But you don't know Marcus. He doesn't think before he acts. Witness this 'rescue' effort."

She stiffened. "It wasn't his fault we went down."

"It's never his fault."

His tone was bitter. Sibling jealousy? Marcus was the youngest, and Harris seemed to carry all the responsibility. But Marcus was changing. Did Harris see that? Or did he not want to?

"A good thing you're injured," she said through her teeth. "Marcus took charge on the ship, made sure I was safe, made sure everyone was safe. I know you don't think he takes initiative, but he took charge. He risked his life to save the others."

"He risks his life all the time, that's what he gets off on. That, and making bad decisions."

She felt like her molars would grind to powder. She rocked back on her heels. "You know, you're ungrateful. I thought you were different when I talked to you on the phone. I thought maybe Marcus saw what he wanted to see when he said you judged him hard. Now I think maybe it's you who only sees what he wants to see."

She rose in one movement and pivoted away, almost stumbling over George, and looked into Marcus's hooded eyes. He'd probably heard all of that. Silently he turned back toward their nest. She followed, her stomach tight in anticipation of what he might say, but he said nothing, just held up the blanket for her to slide beneath. But he made no move to take her back into his arms.

***

Damn, it was getting hard not to fall asleep, even with the pain that throbbed constantly in his leg. Marcus lifted his head from where it rested against the side of the plane and jostled Brylie, whose breathing had slowed.

"Wake up."

"'M awake," she muttered, but he'd lay odds she hadn't been.

The plane was bloody frigid. The wind had died, but he knew from experience that only made the temperature drop. He folded his arm around her shoulders and drew her closer, though he'd been pretty pissed at her for talking to Harris about him earlier. She had no right to talk to his brother—and no business defending him. Harris had been right that she didn't know him. She didn't know what a screw-up he was. She didn't need another screw-up in her life. He should have thought about that before, but hadn't thought anything would happen after their night in Hobart. Now...he couldn't think of anything except their future.

"How long have we been here now?" she asked, turning her face into his throat. Her nose was icy.

"Five hours, just about."

"Probably we should move around to keep warm."

"Check on the others, anyway."

"You could try the satellite phone again, see if you can raise the ship, see if they've heard anything."

They had been able to make a garbled call to the ship to let them know the situation, but hadn't heard back. The phone battery was draining quickly in the cold, and that scared the hell out of him. He pushed back the blanket, then struggled to his feet, grabbing onto the back of the seat when his leg wanted to collapse beneath him. "Christ." He beat his gloved hands against his chest, then reached down to help her to her feet.

"You check on our patients," she said. "Wake up Carl and George. I'll make the call."

Because using the phone meant walking out of the plane to get reception. He opened his mouth to protest, but the way his leg was rebelling, he'd have to let her. He might make it to the end of the plane, but coming back would be a different story. So he'd play nursemaid while she called for help.

He was rousing Carl when she returned up the aisle, shaking her head.

"I could go to the helicopter and use the radio there."

He straightened so fast he hit his head on the overhead compartment, and his leg screamed in agony. "No, you're not. We have the beacons. They'll find us. They're on their way. We just have to wait."

She lifted an eyebrow and he realized he was being the cautious one.

"I can see the helicopter from here," she said.

"Distances are deceiving in this landscape. And if anything happens to you, none of us can come to your aid. We stay here. We wait. Move the bedding over here. We're going to have to use our body heat to help these guys. I can't wake George up."

He could see the tension in her shoulders that told him she wanted to act. He understood that too well, but that she was the healthiest made him uneasy. If rescue didn't arrive soon, she might be required to do something that would put her at risk, and he couldn't protect her.

She moved the bedding to the door of the cockpit, close to the lantern giving off stingy heat. Once she was settled, she roused George enough to get him to eat a power bar and sip some bottled water, while Marcus got Carl to move next to Harris, to keep him warm.

"I wish we had coffee or something," Marcus muttered.

"Have you ever had hypothermia?" she asked, settling into the new nest of blankets, her legs drawn up so she wouldn't jostle Harris's.

He looped his arms around her so her back was against his chest. "Nah. The worst time was when a group of us got stranded on a mountain for a few hours. Storm blew in, rescue couldn't come. We found an outcropping of rock and huddled together. Got to know my mates real well that night."

She shifted so her cheek rested against his shoulder. "You did?"

"Yeah, we, ah, well, the rescuers told us we did the right thing using body heat, keeping our cores warm."

She wriggled her hips between his thighs. "How exactly did you use body heat?"

"We stripped down to our shirts and huddled close, using our coats to cover us up. And we had coffee."

She looked over at Harris, still unconscious despite Marcus's attempts to wake him—including tossing insults at him. "You may have to get to know your brother just as well."

He scowled but nodded. "Carl and George can be on this side, and you, Harris and I can be on the other. Whatever you do, don't go to sleep, all right?"

Marcus insisted Brylie stay on the aisle, closer to the lantern for warmth. As much as he wanted to stretch out beside her, his brother needed her heat more. For a few minutes after crawling under the cotton blankets covered by the space blanket, Marcus actually felt warm. He reached across his brother's body and closed his hand around Brylie's forearm. "Okay?"

"Okay." Her teeth chattered.

"Don't go to sleep."

She nodded. "I know. So talk to me. Tell me about the time you won the bronze."

"Oh, hell." He stroked his fingertips over her sleeve, wishing he could touch her skin, could feel her heart beat against his. "There was nothing special about that run."

"You won the medal."

"Yeah, but it was a run I'd done a hundred times. I just didn't make any mistakes."

"You really didn't have a desire to be the best when you started?"

He chuckled. "I have never in my life had a desire to be the best." If Harris was awake he would confirm that without hesitation.

"Why not?"

"Why?" He laughed through his nose. "It's a hell of a lot of pressure. Who needs it?" He peered through the dim light. "You need it."

She frowned. "So you don't feel that drive in you? Why did you compete?"

"My friends were trying out. I tried out. I made the team. Some of my mates didn't."

She winced. "Did that cause bad blood?"

He shrugged. "Yeah, some. The whole silver-platter thing, you know? If I hadn't tried out, maybe they would have gotten in. Who's to say?"

"Maybe that's why you're not all that thrilled with winning. Guilt?"

He laughed out loud this time. "I've never felt guilty for anything in my life until I met you."

"Maybe you have but just don't know it."

He blew out a dismissive snort. He'd been an egotistical, entitled brat and he knew it. He also knew he didn't want to be that person anymore, didn't want to think about what an ass he'd been. Which was why he didn't like to talk about his snowboarding days. "So anyway, I trained, I developed a run, I executed, I won. Well, came in third."

"And became the bad boy of snowboarding."

He chuckled. "I'd have to get a lot worse to hold that title. Some of those blokes are off their rockers."

"But you're here because you punched someone in the face."

"For being a jackass. I would have done the same if I hadn't been a snowboarder."

"What did he do that made him a jackass?"

"He was hitting on a girl, she didn't want anything to do with him and kept telling him so. He wasn't listening. I thought I'd help him hear what she was saying. He didn't listen to me, either. He swung first and missed. I didn't."

"And you got arrested."

"Wasn't my first time."

"Yeah?" He heard the smile in her voice. "What else?"

"What you'd think. Bad behavior. Vandalism, criminal mischief. No DUIs or drugs, if you're worried about that. Have you ever been arrested?"

She laughed. "No, though I imagine Lily wouldn't have minded seeing me in jail for something or another. I'm surprised she didn't try it."

He linked his gloved hand with hers and wished he could feel her skin. "Not something I would recommend."

"Did you get a boyfriend?" she teased.

It was his turn to laugh. "I wasn't there that long, thanks to Harris here. Couple of hours. I had one picked out, though. Big tattooed guy."

"You would have been cute together."

Something in her voice alarmed him. "Don't go to sleep, Brylie."

"'M not."

"Brylie!" he said sharply.

"I'm awake."

"I'll pinch you."

"Marcus. I'm fine." But her voice was slurred.

He shifted closer against the fuselage. "Get over here. Between me and Harris."

"I don't want to move." Her voice carried a hint of a whine, like a child who didn't want to be put down for a nap. "Besides, he's hurt. He needs our heat."

"He'll get it again after we warm you up. Come here, Brylie."

She shifted and rose, her movements slow, which scared the hell out of him until he realized she was being careful not to jostle Harris. She eased between the brothers and nestled her cold nose against his throat. Her gloved hands slid inside his coat and wrapped around his back.

"You're warm."

He pounded her hard enough to make her pull away to look at him.

"Ow! I'm awake."

"See that you stay that way. You tell me a story now."

"I don't have any good stories. I can't think, Marcus, don't make me think." She snuggled deeper into him.

But he had to make her think. That was the only thing to keep her awake. "Where do you live in the off-season?"

"I told you that the night we met."

"I don't remember."

"Because you had one thing on your mind."

He rubbed his hand down her back. "Can you blame me? Did you see yourself in that outfit?"

"I was wearing jeans and a T-shirt."

"I couldn't take my eyes off of you."

She looked up at him. "Why?"

"I don't know." He shouldn't have said anything. He didn't want to reveal too much, even in the interest of keeping her alert. "All that pretty red hair. I don't usually go for redheads, but it looked so soft."

She reached up to touch it. "My hair."

"And your skin. So smooth. And you looked—sad."

"I didn't think sad was a turn-on."

"Not a turn-on." He shifted and drew her closer. "It just—you asked why I approached you."

"You didn't ask me why I was sad. Which I wasn't."

"I didn't really want to know why—I just didn't want you to be sad anymore."

"So you took me to your room to cheer me up?" Laughter colored her voice.

"Something like that." He brushed his lips over her forehead and felt himself grow hard at the memory of taking her hand in his and leading her into his room. "Why did you come?"

She drew in a breath, like he didn't already know it had been out of the ordinary to accept a man's invitation to go to bed. "I guess I wanted to feel something and you had this look in your eyes that promised I'd definitely feel something."

He chuckled. At least she was awake now. "I hope I lived up to that."

"I'm not indulging in ego-stroking today." She smiled, then ducked her head back under his chin. "And I live in San Francisco. I have a friend with a restaurant there. It's not a grand place and it doesn't pay great, but enough for me to live in the city and rebuild my reputation."

He didn't let himself examine the pang in his stomach at her words. Instead, he said what he would have said to any girl he'd shared a casual night with, like that was all she was to him. "If you want a recommendation when we get back, I can do that. My family's not without some pull."

She stiffened. "I don't want anyone to think I got my reputation by sleeping with the ship's owner."

Huh. She was alert now, and her pride was pricked. He would have gone for that first if he'd known it would work. Still, he regretted taking those measures, losing the softness of her tone, the sweetness of the memory of their night together. "But you work for a friend. Is it that different?"

Before she could answer he heard something outside the plane, and put his hand over her mouth. When she protested, he shushed her, which made her more indignant.

"Listen!" he ordered.

She stilled, and then wriggled again as she heard it, too. Approaching engines. Not a plane, though.

He used the seat to pull himself to his feet—okay, his foot, since his right leg would no longer take his weight, "Snowmobiles," he said.

"That's weird." She'd risen behind him. "They can't carry out injured people on—"

The engines died and Marcus found himself holding his breath waiting to see who had come for them. Brylie tried to push past him, but he held out an arm to hold her back. Something wasn't right. Relief had him slumping his shoulders when Michael and Evan, Jimmy's two friends, stepped through the opening of the plane.

"Thank God you guys are here. We have three injured, one dead—"

"And Marcus hurt his leg when we went down," Brylie added, edging up to stand beside him. "Is a plane or helicopter coming, because I don't think they can ride out on snowmobiles." She motioned to the men behind her.

Unease prickled Marcus's skin. "Why did you guys come?" he asked. "Where did you get snowmobiles?"

"The captain sent us when we lost contact. Didn't you know there were snowmobiles on the ship?" Evan asked. "Hell, you own the ship."

Marcus shook his head. "It just seems—do you have a radio? Call back to the ship and tell them we need an airlift. My brother's in pretty bad shape. So's the co-pilot."

Evan gestured to Michael with a nod of his head, and Michael walked out of the plane.

"The plane's pretty messed up. Did you find everything?" Evan asked.

The cold must have seeped into Marcus's brain, because he didn't understand. "Everything?"

"You know, the ransom and everything."

Alarm flashed along Marcus's nerves as Brylie said, "We didn't even think to look for it. I'm sure it's here somewhere."

"Is that why you're here?" Marcus's question stepped on her last words and he shifted to stand in front of her again as realization bloomed. "You're here for the ransom. Not us. You're the one who was working with the pirates."

"Now." Evan inclined his head. "Why would I team up with people who killed my friends?"

"I heard you." Marcus edged forward, not sure what he'd do, what he could do with his injury. "I heard you talking to them. I didn't recognize your voice at first—all you Yanks sound alike. But you were working with them."

"My friends and I tried to take them down," Evan pointed out.

"So you wouldn't have to split the money so many ways."

"Marcus."

Brylie put her hand on his arm, but he wouldn't be placated. He was right, and he was going to make Evan admit it. "I heard you talking to Hilario."

"Trying to reason with him. Trying to get him to go easy on the passengers. Someone had to do it. You were hiding."

Marcus's temper snapped and he launched himself at the other man. Brylie screamed when his leg collapsed beneath him, and he looked up to see Evan holding a gun, aiming it at Brylie.

"Find the money." Evan ignored Marcus, who sprawled in the aisle, his leg screaming. Shit. Not a hairline fracture anymore.

Brylie stood over him, her shoulders stiff, defiant. "I didn't see anything that could be it. Would it be in a briefcase? A duffel?"

"How the hell should I know?" Evan trained the pistol on Marcus and motioned with the barrel for Marcus to shift out of the way.

Before he could protest, Brylie stepped over him, walking up to Evan as if the gun wasn't there. "I'll look. But you get away from him."

Evan lifted his hands in acquiescence, pistol held loosely, pointing at the ceiling, and Brylie slipped past him.

She moved through the plane, opening compartments he knew she'd been in already when they'd been looking for blankets. Was she just appeasing Evan, or buying time?

Michael stepped back into the plane then. "We've got to go. The plane's nearly here."

What plane? The rescue plane, or did these two have another means of escape planned? Either way, he had to stop them. If he could get off the damned floor. The listing plane made him off-balance, and his leg wouldn't cooperate.

"Maybe this," she said, and Marcus twisted to see her tug something down from an overhead compartment.

Evan stepped forward, gun trained on her again, his other hand extended for the oversized bag she held. Was it the ransom? How much space did—what was it—ten million dollars take up? Had Harris brought that much money? And wouldn't he be pissed if these two assholes made off with it?

Brylie edged toward Evan, holding the bag by its handles, chest high as if to counter the weight. He was confused by her method for a minute, and then she swung the bag, hard, over the top of the seat, knocking Evan's gun hand aside. He didn't release the weapon. It fired, the sound filling the small space. Marcus lunged for Evan's knees and took him down, hard, onto his back, before reaching for the gun. Shit, the guy was strong, straining to raise his weapon. Marcus struggled to pin his hand to the floor. Brylie cried out in alarm. Marcus looked up to see Michael grasp her by the hair and drag her to her feet. She released the bag to grab for his hands, to release the pressure on her hair. Michael dropped her, snatched up the bag and ran toward the exit.

***

Brylie gained her feet and sprinted after him. *Shit.* An engine kicked to life and Marcus's heart leapt to his throat. Did Michael have Brylie? Wresting the gun from Evan, Marcus swung the weapon hard against his opponent's head and felt him slump. Gripping the gun in his left hand so he could pull himself up with his right, he launched himself after Brylie.

He stumbled out into the whiteness to see her astride the second snowmobile, trying to crank it on. A few yards away, Michael was making his get-away in a spray of snow.

Ten million dollars. Only money, but to get it back might show Harris he wasn't a screw-up after all. He dragged himself toward the snowmobile, pulled himself on behind her, reached around her for the handles and kicked it on while she fumbled with snow-goggles. They shot off after Michael, the vehicle kicking over the uneven terrain a few times before Brylie guided it to a smoother path.

"What the hell are we doing?" he shouted at her.

"Getting your money back."

"Getting ourselves killed," he corrected, and closed his hands over hers on the handles.

Ahead of them, the spray of snow from Michael's snowmobile disappeared. Marcus let off the throttle and their engine slowed. Where the hell was the other snowmobile? A terrible sound carried over the snow, a sound of metal crumpling, and then silence. A plume of smoke rose ahead of them, in a dip in the landscape. Marcus started toward it, guiding the snowmobile on a rise. He caught sight of the crevasse seconds before the explosion rocked across the ice. He swore and twisted hard, skidding sideways as he felt the vibration of the ice cracking. No way could Michael have survived the explosion, even if he'd survived the fall into the crevasse. He and Brylie had to get out of here before the cracks in the ice reached them.

The engine sputtered beneath them, and Brylie's body was tight with resistance as she tried to turn them back the way they'd come.

"Too late, Brylie," he said, close to her ear. "Sorry. It's too late. He's gone."

Afraid to take the time to look behind him, he ran the engine full-out toward the plane. And there, just over the edge of the mountain, he saw the landing lights of a rescue plane.

CHAPTER TEN

Brylie sat on the end of the gurney in the emergency department. She was marginally warmer than she'd been on the rescue plane, where the EMTs had worked hard on George and Harris while she, Carl and Marcus drank coffee and huddled in blankets. Marcus hadn't told them about his leg—she'd had to point it out to the techs. Once they'd reached Hobart, the five of them had been separated for medical attention. Brylie wanted to find Marcus first, then see how Harris and George were doing. She'd spoken on the phone to her father, but he wouldn't be in port for two more days.

"Excuse me." She tried to catch the attention of a passing nurse, but was ignored. Again.

"That's not the way to do it."

Marcus twitched aside the curtain around the gurney and grinned. He leaned on a cane with the hand that wasn't in a sling, and his injured leg was in a temporary inflatable cast. He shouldn't look so delicious with that lop-sided grin, but boy, did he. He turned on his good foot and raised his cane to stop the next woman in scrubs who passed.

"I'd like to take my girl out of here. Is she ready to go?"

The woman looked from Marcus to Brylie, while Brylie focused on Marcus's wording. The woman crossed to look at Brylie's chart, then her vitals.

"Her core temperature isn't quite where we want it to be yet."

"Believe me when I tell you I know how I can warm her up. Let her come home with me, okay?"

The nurse glanced again from one to the other, but this time a twinkle lit her eyes. "What do you think, Miss Winston? Would you like to go home with this young man and try his method?"

Brylie looked at Marcus and her breath caught. "Yes, I think I would. In the interest of science and all."

The nurse—her nametag read Yolie—laughed. "I'll go get a doctor to sign off on you."

"How are Harris and George?" she asked Marcus when Yolie left and he stepped closer to her gurney.

"George is still in surgery. Harris is in ICU, being closely monitored though they're hopeful he'll have a full recovery, and I'm pretty determined to get out of here before the family descends."

"You could have gone without me, you know."

He stroked a lock of hair back from her face. "No. I couldn't have. You were brave as hell out there, hell, this whole time. You're an amazing woman, Brylie."

Behind him, Yolie sighed, holding the chart to her chest. Marcus stepped back and let Brylie sign the discharge papers, then looped the cane over his arm and hooked his good arm over her shoulders as they walked out of the hospital.

***

The cab ride to the hotel was short and Brylie's pulse drummed. It had been one thing to go to his room before she knew him. It had been another to turn to him on the ship. But what choice was she making here, going to a hotel room when danger had passed, when they were ready to get on with their lives? Was he really someone she wanted to let into her real life? Was she someone who would fit in his?

Why was she overthinking what was probably only good-bye sex?

She waited nearby as he checked in, feeling awkward without luggage, still wearing her layers from the trip to Antarctica, feeling grimy in the marble-floored hotel. She glimpsed herself in the mirror behind the check-in, saw the distaste in the eyes of the clerk, and wished Marcus looked half as disheveled as she did. But no, he looked scruffy and gorgeous.

"The room has a big tub?" he asked the clerk.

The young woman widened her eyes. "It's a nice size."

"Big enough for two?" he asked, and the clerk blushed.

"I'm sure you'll find a way, sir."

"I'm sure I will." He turned to Brylie and inclined his head toward the way to the gift shop.

"What?" she asked, afraid she knew.

"Left the condoms on the ship, didn't we?"

"I don't want everyone to know what we're doing." Her cheeks heated as she said the words.

"No?" Setting the cane down, he pressed his hand to the small of her back and brought her to him, covering her mouth with his.

The kiss seared her from lips to toes, the heat stopping along the way to tighten her nipples and make her sex throb. She curved her hand around the back of his head as he glided his tongue along hers and slid his hand beneath the hem of her sweatshirt so that his thumb circled the small of her back. More heat, more tingles of desire and she pushed her hips into his.

He lifted his head and grinned. "Now they know what we'll be doing." He stepped back, taking her hand and guiding her into the gift shop.

While he was selecting the large pack, she spotted a table with discounted sweatshirts—something clean to put on her body. But she didn't have money with her and she wouldn't ask him to buy it for her.

But he was paying attention. "One of those, too," he told the clerk, gesturing. "And do you have any panties that aren't granny sized?"

She turned and saw him pointing to the packs of underwear hanging behind the counter. The young girl shook her head, blushing. "But we could send someone out for some, if you'd like, Mr. Devlin."

"Yes, please. A size—" He turned to Brylie for confirmation.

"Six."

"Yes, sir. Color preference?"

He hadn't taken his eyes off of Brylie, and she wanted to squirm under the attention. "I'm partial to white. Charge it to the room, will you?" He looped the bag containing condoms, toothbrushes and toothpaste over his injured hand, motioned to Brylie to select her sweatshirt, and headed for the elevators.

"You do rich guy very well. 'Charge it to the room, will you?'"

"Yeah?"

"Just a different side of you, I guess. Unexpected."

He stepped into the elevator. "Good or bad?"

Since she was tingling from her knees up, she'd say good, but not to him. "Just different."

He leaned against the elevator wall and drew her beside him to make room for the family that joined them. She twisted to look at him.

"Do you own this hotel?"

The family turned, too, and color darkened his cheeks. "Ah." He nodded. "My family."

Right. She'd forgotten how wealthy he was. How powerful, even as the younger son. Nerves skittered over the tingles as her balance slipped. She didn't want a man who held so much power. Hadn't that put her in a bad spot before? She needed someone who was her equal.

But not now. Now she was going to let him treat her like a princess.

The family exited the elevator before they did, and she half-expected him to pull her into his arms. Instead, he breathed out a sigh and linked his fingers through hers. When the doors opened again, he heaved away from the wall, balancing on his cane, and drew her down the hall to the room. She had only a moment to observe the elegance, the leathers and jewel colors, before he threaded his fingers through her hair and kissed her, his lips gentle, soft.

"Want to check out the bathroom?"

She did. Funny how she could feel so gross after bring so cold. And when she walked into the porcelain and chrome opulence, she felt even grimier. Marcus hobbled over and turned on the water in the huge gleaming tub, definitely big enough for both of them. Then, bracing his weight on the cane, he motioned for her to peel off her sweatshirt.

She did so gratefully, tossing it aside. He grinned, his eyes gleaming, warming her more than the blankets she'd huddled under on the plane. She reached for the button of her jeans, not believing she was even thinking about a striptease. Still, she held his gaze as she unsnapped the button and shimmied the cotton fabric down over her silk longjohns. Giddiness bubbled up in her—she'd never done such a silly thing. Never felt comfortable enough with a man to do such a thing.

She jammed her hands on her hips. "How's this, thermals and flannel? Does this work for you?"

"More than you know." He stretched his good hand to her but she waved it off.

"Not done." She started at the bottom of her flannel shirt and unbuttoned slowly, peeling back the fabric to reveal—more thermals. "How's this?"

He sat on the edge of the tub. "Sexiest thing I've ever seen."

She tossed her hair, turned her back to him and peeled the flannel down her arms so she wore only her form-fitting thermals. She turned to face him and lifted the t-shirt over her head, then skimmed down the pants, taking the socks with them. By the time she straightened, he'd removed the inflatable cast and moved in. He tugged her naked body against his, the roughness of his clothes adding another layer to her arousal as his mouth covered hers, his kiss hot, tongue stroking, his fingers digging into her upper arm, his arousal growing against her stomach. She slid her hands under his sweatshirt, his corduroy shirt and his cotton thermal shirt and found the waist of the scrub pants the hospital had given him, after cutting his pants off because of his swollen leg. She closed her fingers around his cock and took his moan of pleasure into her mouth.

He broke the kiss and unlooped his sling from his head, then stripped his clothes off in short order. He backed toward the tub, his grip on her left arm a little stronger as he worked for balance. She waited until he settled into the tub, stepping in with his good leg first, then he motioned to her. She eased into the warm water, closing her eyes at the sensation, and lowered herself over him, straddling his hips, her hands on his shoulders. She leaned forward to kiss him. Their mouths found each other as his hand glided down her back to curve over her bottom, drawing her closer, over him. His touch teased the inside of her thigh. She let her head fall back as his fingers circled closer to where she wanted it most.

"We didn't." He pressed a kiss to the side of her throat. "Bring." The curve of her shoulder. "The condoms."

"I'll go get them," she volunteered, pulling back to rise, causing the water to slosh.

His grip tightened on her thigh. "Not yet." His hand moved between her legs and she gasped, pushing her hips into his touch. A chuckle rumbled in his chest at her eagerness, and his pace increased.

She tensed over him, and then heat pulsed through her, from his stroking fingers to her extremities, setting fire to those tingles and burning them out, leaving her limp against his chest.

He stroked her hair against her cheek, her shoulder, her back. She worked up all her energy to turn her head to kiss his neck. Moments passed before she became aware of his erection still throbbing against her belly.

"I'll get the condoms as soon as my bones grow back," she said against his skin, tasting him, nipping his earlobe.

"Warming up?"

"Mm." She could go to sleep right here, draped over him, but that would hardly be fair.

"Turn around," he urged, and she did, careful not to jostle his leg.

She sat between his parted thighs with a sigh, leaning back against his chest and watching him lazily as he picked up a lush washcloth and trailed it over her skin. She moaned as the warm water caressed her. His touch was gentle, reverent, as he washed her shoulders, arms, breasts, belly, lower.

"Lean forward," he murmured, and turned on the hand-held sprayer to wash her hair.

His touch on her scalp as he soaped her hair was erotic as hell, and her arousal returned, a slow throb this time.

After he rinsed the shampoo away, she turned, her hands on his chest, his erection against her stomach. She reached for the cloth to return the favor, but he caught her wrist. She looked up to see his jaw tight.

"The bed."

Yes. She rose from the tub, reaching for a lush towel from the bar and wrapping it around herself while he watched, his gaze hot. Yeah, she wasn't cold any more.

"Need a hand?" She was surprised at the breathlessness of her own voice.

"You're going to have to be on top." Positioning his weight strategically to accommodate his injuries, he heaved himself out of the tub.

She let her gaze linger on his sex and smiled. "I have no problem with that."

Tucking the towel beneath her arm, she led the way into the bedroom.

He followed, and stretched out on the huge bed, bandaged arm above his head. "Do your worst."

She knelt on the bed, still wrapped in the towel, and bent to kiss his mouth, lingering only briefly as she slid her hands down his still-damp chest to close around his erection. She followed the path with her mouth, nuzzling in his chest hair, nibbling his nipple before descending over his flat stomach, tense now with anticipation. She kept her gaze on him as she closed her lips around him. He flexed his hips and groaned as she dragged her tongue along his length. The effect made her feel powerful and sexy, so she repeated the caress.

"Brylie." He threaded his fingers through her hair and tugged lightly. "I want to be in you. I want to touch you."

Her own body throbbing with the same need, she released him and rose over him, letting the towel fall away. His nostrils flared in appreciation as she edged her knees alongside his hips, reaching for a condom from the nearby table. Once he was sheathed, she guided him to her and plunged down.

God, he made her feel so full, and she took a moment to adjust before she moved, rising and falling slowly along the length of him, savoring the stretch and clasp of her body around him, the friction delicious. He cupped his good hand over her hip, guiding her, holding her as he lifted into her. She hadn't realized she was so close to another orgasm, but now she could almost grasp it, her whole body straining toward it. Her thrusts were frantic, searching for the rhythm that would give it to her, when he added his touch.

"Brylie, look at me," he urged through the haze of pleasure that floated around her. "Look at me."

She opened her eyes and met his gaze. He anchored her hips, pistoning his own beneath her. Harder, deeper, faster.

She spiraled into the orgasm, reeled with it, cried out with it, heard his own echoing cry through the mist of her own pleasure, and she floated bonelessly to lay on his chest.

"Warm now," she managed.

He chuckled softly, his hand trailing up and down the indentation at the base of her spine, drawing out the tingles she thought he'd obliterated with that orgasm.

"We are really good at this," she murmured.

"You're not going to run out on me again, are you?" He pressed a kiss to her forehead.

"Couldn't if I wanted to." She nestled her head against his shoulder, her fingers playing in his chest hair. He shifted her to deal with the condom, then settled her back beside her. His movements slow as he drew the covers over them. Within moments, the steadiness of his breathing lulled her to sleep.

***

Marcus slipped back into bed after taking a pill to relieve the throbbing in his leg and hand. He'd been surprised to see early morning light coming through the windows when the pain woke him. That meant they'd been asleep for fourteen hours, maybe longer, since they'd arrived yesterday afternoon.

Which explained why he was so bloody hungry. But he didn't want to wake Brylie just yet.

Things had changed since the last time they were in a hotel room together. That time they'd both been looking for an escape. This time—he didn't know what they were looking for. He just knew he wasn't done looking yet, wasn't ready to walk away. She'd been amazing on the ship, braver and stronger than any woman ever he'd known. She'd made him feel braver and stronger. He liked the person he was when he was with her.

He'd thought maybe he'd look into being in charge of security now, and hit the seas with her, but the season here was over. Their cruise had been the last until next December. Would she return to her friend's restaurant in San Francisco?

The idea hit him hard enough to knock the breath out of him. He knew how to keep her close enough to figure out what it was she made him feel.

A few hours later, he woke her up with a smack to her ass. "Wake up, lazybones."

She stretched like a cat beneath the blankets and squinted up at him through a tangle of red hair. "What is it?"

"I have a surprise for you. Get dressed."

***

Brylie tucked her hands into her front pockets as she stared up at the brick building with the large plate glass windows looking out on the street that had very little traffic—lots of empty buildings, though many looked to be in the middle of renovations. Marcus rocked on his cane beside her.

"What is it?" she asked finally.

"A restaurant. Come on in."

He pulled out a key with a tag on it, unlocked the door and pushed it open for her to precede him. She did, cautiously. The place was spotless, with dark wood floors and brick walls, roomy enough for two dozen tables. A mahogany bar ran down the side of the wall, with mirrors behind to open up the space, and recessed lighting to illuminate the shelves that would hold the liquor. He guided her to the kitchen, which was open and spectacular. She could already envision the stainless steel appliances that would line the walls, could already see the layout, could already hear the sounds of the staff rushing to meet orders.

Marcus watched her, his eyes bright. Her stomach tightened.

"What is this?" she asked, though she was pretty sure she knew.

"Your restaurant. You could name it Brylie's, paint it right across the window there." He gestured. "The neighborhood's not much yet, but they're revitalizing, you know, to bring in the tourist trade. I think it would be an amazing place. My sister told me about the plans for the neighborhood when I called and—"

She held up a hand, his words flowing over her, making it impossible for her to process them. "My restaurant?"

"Right. You were saving money and you wanted to run your own place and I thought this would be the place." His words faded. "You don't like it."

"I—" She leaned back against the pass-through and folded her arms over her chest. "Why?"

The pleasure on his face faded, too, and she felt like the world's biggest bitch. "I thought that would be obvious."

"What I'm thinking—that can't be. So spell it out for me."

He squirmed. "I—thought it would make you happy."

"Marcus. The fancy hotel room made me happy. The great big bathtub, the great big bed. This—" She stretched her arms out to encompass the building, her voice bouncing off the brick walls, her pulse thundering, a combination of fear and sorrow. He was giving her this place? And then? She'd had the rug snatched from under her before. "This is something else."

"You're right." This time he folded his arms and leaned back against the brick wall. "It is something else. It's—I don't want you to go back to the States."

She stepped back. He was asking her to stay, have a future. And when she looked at him, her heart turned over. So why was she so scared? "My life is there."

"What life? You work in someone else's restaurant, you said yourself you work and go home. What are you going home to?"

She regretted those confessions now. "My dreams."

His eyes narrowed. "Of owning a restaurant."

A world-class restaurant. One that would make her the toast of San Francisco. Not—a bistro in Hobart. "I don't own it. You do."

"So?"

"So when you get tired of me, or of this, what happens? I'm out on my ass and having to start all over again."

"The asshole in New York?"

"Was my boss."

His forehead smoothed and his eyes went flat in an expression she'd seen when he spoke to Harris. Masking pain. "You think I'm like that?"

She couldn't take that chance. "Marcus, you hardly know me. What if we do this," she flipped her finger between the two of them, "and you decide you don't like the real me, the everyday me? You'll be invested in this restaurant and can't just walk away and you'll end up hating me."

"I won't."

She shook her head. "I can't depend on anyone else. I need to depend on myself, find my own success or it will never be mine."

"Bullshit," he said, and she pivoted. "Bullshit. We got through that because we knew how to work together. We were good together. I'd let you do what you want in the restaurant—you know better than I do. And if it goes to hell between us, well, we can have that written into the contract, some kind of out. I'm sure a lawyer can come up with a reasonable solution. But I wouldn't have done this if I didn't have some faith here." He uncrossed his arms and held out a hand to her. "Do you have faith?"

Temptation tugged. It was a pretty place, in a pretty town, and the gesture—she couldn't even call it a gesture because it was so huge—was so generous, just because he wanted her to be happy.

"I never thought you'd want anything past—what we have."

His jaw tightened. "Is that why you slept with me? Because you figured once we got back to Australia we'd be done?"

She felt her face heat. "It occurred to me."

A disbelieving smile canted his lips. "And you're afraid that I'm the one who'll walk away?"

"You don't even know what you want in your life. Why would I think we could have a future? I can't give anyone else that control, ever again."

"So, I take it back." He lifted his hands in surrender. "I thought I was giving you something you wanted." His jaw tightened and he pushed himself away from the wall. "You say you want control, but you're still giving him that control."

She drew back as if he'd slapped her.

He leaned heavily on his cane. "You're letting what he did to you make your decisions now. It's making you scared to trust, scared to let go of any control."

She squared her shoulders, feeling completely vulnerable because of his words, wishing she had a purse or bag or something to use as a shield between them.

He wanted her. But for how long? A future with him was out of her control, something she couldn't bear.

He'd gotten her through the worst ordeal of her life with his bravery and his humor. She just didn't have room for love in her life, didn't have room for a man who didn't even know what he wanted to do with his own life.

"I can't. I'm sorry, Marcus. No one has ever done anything like this for me before, but I can't."

His lips thinned and he bounced the keys in his hand. He inclined his head toward the door. "Let's go, then."

She hesitated. "There's—really nothing I need at the hotel. Maybe I should just get a cab from here."

He looked at her for a long moment, then nodded, tightened his grip on his cane, and walked away.

***

The Ice Queen was due into port tomorrow, otherwise Brylie would have flown back to San Francisco immediately, put as much distance between herself and her insane longing for Marcus as she could. She'd tendered her resignation with the cruise line, and waited for her father's arrival in a hotel nowhere near the one where she'd stayed with Marcus, while she mourned the way she'd hurt him.

Hurt herself. No man had ever wanted to give her something like that without wanting something for himself. He hadn't asked for anything from her—only wanted to give her what she wanted because it made her happy. He'd even offered her a solution for an exit if their relationship failed, and had done so good-naturedly, as he'd done everything. And she'd shoved it back in his face.

She tried to tell herself that he would want something from her eventually, but the short amount of time they'd spent together told her he wouldn't. If she didn't give him what he needed, he might move on, but he wouldn't ask her to hand his gift back.

But she knew that she couldn't live with either of those choices, and she was too jaded to believe in happy endings. She'd never witnessed one outside of movies—and even those were written that way.

She couldn't, however, stop herself from visiting Harris, to see how he was faring. She'd depended on him a lot when she'd been on the ship, when Marcus had sacrificed himself to the terrorists to keep her and the other passengers safe.

She made sure Marcus wasn't around when she approached Harris's room. This felt too much like New York and her fear of running into Ethan in those weeks following her humiliation, before she could get out of town.

But no Marcus in sight, and when she walked into Harris's room, she knew why. He had his computer set up on the table in front of him and was haranguing someone on the phone while a nurse urged him to be quiet. His demeanor changed when he saw Brylie, and he actually smiled as he gave the person on the other end a list of orders and hung up.

"Feeling better, I see." She stopped at the foot of the bed.

"I've been better. Would be better if these people would let me get back to work." He sent the nurse a glare.

"I'm sure they wish they could." Brylie offered the young woman a sympathetic smile as she left.

"Where's my brother?"

Her stomach tightened though she'd expected the question. "I don't know. We parted ways."

"Figures he'd blow it."

"No, he—he was great. I was the one who walked away."

"If he's so great, why did you walk away?"

"I'm going back to the States as soon as I see my father, so there was no point dragging it out." She squirmed under his scrutiny, and admitted that part of her wanted him to prompt her further. That traitorous part wanted to talk about Marcus, who she hadn't been able to get out of her head. "Has he not come to see you?"

Harris scowled. "He's been a couple of times, the ungrateful boof head. Always walks out in the middle of an argument."

"Arguing about what?" She sat on the edge of a chair near the window.

"His worthless life, that's what. Almost thirty years old and doesn't know what he wants to do. Bought a restaurant with my sister's help and now he's looking to sell it after only two days. Thinks he wants to be in security, now. What the hell does he know about security?"

"He kept a lot of people safe on the ship."

Harris shot her an annoyed glance. "Figures you'd stick up for him. Women always do. My wife, for instance. Tells me just because he's not like me doesn't make him a bad person. Hell, sometimes she tells me it makes him a better person."

Turned out she didn't want to talk about Marcus, especially not how other women stood up for him. "I'm sorry we couldn't get you the money back."

He lifted his eyebrows. "What money?"

Brylie tensed in surprise. She knew they were wealthy, but to forget about ten million dollars blown into confetti— "The ransom money."

He scowled. "There was no ransom money. Not what they asked for, anyway. We know how to deal with people like that. It was a few thousand real, and several million counterfeit."

"So why did you accompany it?"

"To make it look real. Do you think a person in charge of that much money would just send it with lackeys?"

"And you nearly got yourself killed."

"That was unforeseen. In any case, that's the position Marcus wants now."

"I think he'd be good at it."

"Until he gets bored."

That Harris and she had the same concerns about Marcus's level of commitment irritated her. She felt like she should have more faith in him. One of them should, anyway. "So how are you feeling? Getting out soon?"

"Tomorrow, they say."

"It's going to be a long day for them." Brylie inclined her head toward the nurses' station.

"I'll leave them alone if they leave me alone."

She stood and crossed to the bed to kiss his cheek. "Thank you for everything. And don't be so hard on Marcus."

"He never should have let you walk away. You're the best thing that could happen to him."

She shook her head, smiling sadly. "I wouldn't want to change who he is." And she would, with her constant expectations that he would leave her. "If you're ever in San Francisco…"

Harris made a face. "Why would I ever want to do that?"

She pinched his arm and walked out.

***

The Ice Queen came in that night and Brylie spent the evening with her father fussing over her. She'd avoided meeting him at the dock because she didn't want to deal with all the passengers, but when he met her for dinner, he told her that Marcus had been there.

A twinge went through her. She was both grateful to have avoided him and proud of him for being able to do something she couldn't.

"I think he was looking for you," her father said. "I thought you two would be together."

"We parted ways a few days ago." Had he been looking for her? What would he say to her after the way she left him? She was too embarrassed to know what she'd say to him.

Her father didn't pursue it, and she was grateful. "He said he's going to be working with security for the line now, based here."

"His brother told me he wanted the job."

"His brother? Harris?" Her father raised his eyebrows. "You've been keeping some big company."

"He was on the plane that crashed. I helped take care of him and wanted to make sure he was recovering."

"When are you going back to San Francisco?"

"Tomorrow. I just wanted to say good-bye."

"Well, it won't be long until next summer."

"Dad, I'm not coming back. I quit the line. I'm going to keep working in San Francisco and earn the money for my restaurant that way." It would take much longer, but she wouldn't work for Marcus.

Her father pursed his lips. "I hate to see you running again."

"Running?"

"Running away from your troubles. You ran here to get away from New York. You're running back to San Francisco because of what happened here."

"I go back to San Francisco at the end of every season," she reminded him. "I just—I know what I want. Marcus isn't it."

"Marcus?" Her father sat back in his chair. "I was talking about the hostage situation. What about Marcus?"

Her face heated. "We got—close during the time on the ship. He thought maybe it could be a romance." She couldn't bring herself to tell her father about the restaurant because he'd think her a fool for not jumping on it. He'd seen how hard she'd worked to save the money for her own place, and to have it handed to her—he wouldn't understand why she had to walk away.

"And you didn't."

"I don't think I'm built for that. I need too much control of the situation. I certainly wouldn't want to end up like you and Mom."

"Your mother and I had problems like all couples do. But we didn't know how to talk, how to work together. She thought keeping her hopes and dreams from me would make me happy, but all it did was make her resentful and miserable. By the time I learned what she was thinking, it was too late. Too much damage had been done."

"What would you have changed to make her dreams come true?"

He met her gaze. "Anything. I miss her every day. It's hell being alone, Brylie, even when you feel like the most independent person on the planet. There's nothing like sharing your life with someone who wants to share it with you, who wants to make you happy and see you succeed."

How could he know about Marcus and what he'd offered her? Did he know her so well? And why had she walked away from a man who understood her, even though he'd known her such a short time?

Because she hadn't believed it was possible he could know her. She'd been afraid to believe. But now—now she was afraid to walk away.

She stood and kissed her father's cheek. "Thanks for dinner."

"You're leaving? So soon?"

"I have some things to take care of. And I don't think I'll be going too far."

***

She had the cab stop down the block from the restaurant. The street was well-lit with new cast-iron light poles every few feet. She hurried down to the place when she saw the light on through the plate glass window.

And stopped short to see Marcus inside at the bar, his arm around a slender brunette. Her heart seized when he laughed and let the other woman go in order to pour a glass of wine from a familiar looking bottle. One like they'd shared on board The Ice Queen. She pivoted to turn away, hating that she'd been right about his attention span, that she'd been right about believing the worst in him.

But just then she caught sight of the brunette's face, the familiar line of nose and jaw. She'd seen that jaw on Harris, the nose on Marcus. And the flash of blue-gray eyes...

His sister. She had to be. The resemblance was too strong.

Marcus stood and her attention snapped to him. Their gazes met through the window. Her urge to flee tensed the muscles in her legs, especially when she saw no welcome in his face as he limped toward the door.

"Brylie. Come meet my sister Maggie. She helped me pick out the place." He motioned to the "For Sale" sign in the window. "She's helping me put it up for sale, too. Just thought I'd have one drink here before."

He didn't ask why she was here, and she hated the flatness in his voice. No accusation, no emotion at all. She missed the inflections he always used when he spoke, the ones that gave no doubt what he was thinking, what he was feeling. He didn't hide much. She stepped inside hesitantly, glad to have her purse to hold onto, to use as a barrier this time.

"Want a glass of wine?" Maggie asked from the bar, her tone even less friendly than Marcus's.

She shook her head. "I'd—like to talk to Marcus."

Maggie started for the door but Marcus held his hand up to stop her, though he didn't take his gaze from Brylie. "We'll go outside."

The better to give her the bum's rush, no doubt. Not that she could blame him. She walked out the door ahead of him, her grip on her purse so tight that her knuckles were white. And everything she'd planned to say vanished under the intensity of his gaze.

"I came to apologize."

The words didn't ease the crease in his brow at all. "Wanted to make peace before you head back to the States?"

"Actually, no. I'm not going back."

His brows lifted. "No? What about your hopes and dreams?"

"It turns out you were right. I have nothing back there. I have nothing here—not yet, but I think I can build something here if I had a second chance." Why was this all coming out so wrong, so cold, so vague?

He folded his arms and inclined his head toward the storefront. "So you changed your mind? You want this, then?"

"No! Yes. I mean—not the way you think. Not the way…" She turned away and pushed her hand through her hair. If he'd just stop looking at her like that, she could get her thoughts together. But the intensity in his gaze made her believe he'd never forgive her. She had to take the chance that he would. She angled her chin up to meet his gaze. "I don't want you to be my boss."

"Fair enough." He nodded toward the "For Sale" sign.

"But I don't—I never should have walked away. I don't want to walk away from you. You scared me, Marcus."

He braced his hand against the brick façade of the building. "You faced terrorists for a week. That didn't scare you."

"It did, but not like you did. I knew that would end, and I wanted it to. But this—you and me—I'm scared it *will* end. I don't—I don't let myself trust."

He snorted out a laugh.

She scowled. At least his expression had changed. "I hate that about myself. And I hate that I let my fears hurt you."

He straightened. "Brylie. I bought you a restaurant to make you happy. I didn't want anything from it but that. And you walked away because you were a coward. The woman I knew on The Ice Queen was no coward. Neither was the woman who kept my brother alive on the continent. I thought you had balls. I was wrong."

Her face was hot as she angled her chin up. "Does my coming back here count for anything? Because it was a damned hard thing to do, facing you again after walking out."

He inclined his head. "Did you know I would be here?"

"Harris told me, after I didn't find you at your hotel."

His frown relaxed. "You went to Harris?"

She tucked a loose strand of hair behind her ear. "Just so you know, he thought I was an idiot for trying to find you."

"But he still told you where I was."

"After I convinced him that I'd made a mistake."

"By walking away from a free restaurant."

She'd been afraid he'd see it like that. "The restaurant can rot. By walking away from a man who understands me and makes me laugh and makes me scream. By walking away from a man who wants to make me happy and keep me safe, even though he's never wanted responsibility for another person. I thought if you could change that much, I can too. I can trust that I can turn to you when things are good and when things get hard and I can believe that we can hold onto each other and have a future." She stepped forward and risked touching him for the first time. His cheek was warm and bristly and familiar, and he didn't move away from her hand. "I want to be the woman you think I am. I want to be the woman you can love."

He covered her hand with his. "You are that woman, Brylie. Believe it. I do."

She leaned in and he captured her mouth in a kiss that promised faithfulness and a future she could believe in. When they broke apart, he took her hand and led her into the restaurant, yanking down the "For Sale" sign on the way.

THE END

ABOUT THE AUTHOR

MJ Fredrick knows about chasing dreams. Twelve years after she completed her first novel, she signed her first publishing contract. Now she divides her days between teaching elementary music, and diving into her own writing—traveling everywhere in her mind, from Belize to Honduras to Africa to the past.

She's a four-time Golden Heart Award finalist, and she won the 2009 Eppie Award with *Hot Shot* and the 2011 Epic Award with *Breaking Daylight*. Her other romantic suspense titles are *Beneath the Surface*, *Guarded Hearts* and *Don't Look Back*. Her contemporary romances are *Where There's Smoke*, *Something to Talk About*, *Road Signs*, *Three Days, Two Nights*, *Star Power* and *Bull by the Horns*.

Made in the USA
Lexington, KY
19 March 2012